LOVE'S WAY

Other recent Walker romances by Joan Smith
Lovers' Vows
Lace for Milady
Aurora
Dame Durden's Daughter
Imprudent Lady

LOVE'S WAY
═══ Joan Smith ═══

WALKER AND COMPANY
NEW YORK

First published in the United States of America in 1982 by the Walker Publishing Company, Inc.

Published simultaneously in Canada by John Wiley & Sons Canada, Limited, Rexdale, Ontario.

ISBN: 0-8027-0702-5

Library of Congress Catalog Card Number: 81-69708

Printed in the United States of America

10 9 8 7 6 5 4 3 2 1

To Robin and Terry Smith

= 1 =

IF I WERE rich, I would never mend another stitch in my life. I would lie in bed till ten in the mornings, eat strawberries all summer long, have seven gowns with blonde lace, a different colour for every day of the week, and a sable-lined cape for winter. But I am not, so I shall hurry and get Edward's shirt patched up in time to give my aunt some help with peeling the turnips for dinner. Strawberries have a way of turning into turnips here at Ambledown, and blonde lace into well-worn muslin. Still, we are rich in the things that matter: history, health, memories, and dreams. Especially dreams. You never crave a thing with the same gusto once it is actually attainable. And if you *must* have a thing whether you want it or no, you develop a lively distaste for it. Which brings us to Tom Carrick, though I should not perhaps call him an "it."

He is my suitor. He came to call last night and declared himself — made a formal offer of marriage, which I am graciously and reluctantly considering as I sit in the hot sun, mending my brother's shirt and dreaming of strawberries.

I say it is primarily my brother Edward's fault that I am in this pickle. If he were a normal brother, he would have taken Ambledown in hand when Papa died and made us a good living from it. He was at Oxford at the time, however, which is how *I* fell into the temporary role of estate manageress. When he came down two years later, a graduate, he was much too well educated to know anything practical, having turned poet instead. Our fortunes declined apace. The Barwicks, once the second most influential family in the neighbourhood, outpaced

1

only by the Gambles at Carnforth Hall, fell into obscurity. A Barwick ancestor sat in Parliament for Westmoreland as long ago as the fourteenth century. Another fought the Scots at Flodden Fields in 1513, bringing glory to the name. The original farm house, squat, plain, and square, had been grandified into a mansion by a Tudor Barwick in the late sixteenth century. In fact, we have still intact on the premises a pele-tower, used as a look-out post against invaders some four hundred years ago. We use it to store old lumber, with a bachelor farm hand having his quarters on the second story.

Poetry is at the bottom of all our misfortunes. I knew virtually nothing of sheep farming when I took over, whereas Edward had worked with Papa, it always being understood he would take over the place one day. Instead he took into his head to go dragging over to Rydal Mount, where Mr. Wordsworth has set up a colony of rhymesters, to spend his afternoons at the master's feet. At night, he sits cudgelling his brain over sonnets, while I am left to juggle pounds and pence in the never-ending battle to keep a roof over our heads. All this is bad enough, but on top of it, he has lately begun talking of marriage to a perfectly ineligible lady, with not so much as a sou to her name. Of course, she is wildly romantical, her life fraught with unsolvable problems. She shares (or pretends to share) his infatuation with poetry. I do not actually know any perfectly sane, normal people who *regularly* read poetry, when I stop to consider it. Perhaps it is an aberration, like gambling.

I first came to suspect this passion was simmering when Lady Emily began calling on me this past spring. We are neighbours, she living at Carnforth Hall a few miles away, but as she is not far from a decade younger than myself, we were never what one could call real friends. Her papa is a top-lofty earl, who seldom showed his nose in the district for more than a few months a year until he became old and ill. We saw little of Lady Emily until Edward let his curls grow long, took to wearing a Belcher kerchief at his neck and scrambling over the fells like a sheep. All this was done to honour his Muse, you understand. Such antics invoked some of our neighbours to ridicule, some to pity. Lady Emily thinks him a positive charm.

2

Her first pretext for calling on us was to deliver a basket of sour little green oranges, which she informed us would be ideal for making spice balls but 'were a little sour for eating'. She need hardly have told us. She was not long in the saloon before she began asking after Edward. She had to make two more calls before she 'accidentally' caught him in one morning. It was an overcast day, making fell climbing and riding to Rydal Mount ineligible. We were honoured with a green goose and a sack of spongey apples on those two occasions. Aunt Nora was urging the friendship on me as a great thing for the family's lagging dignity. It quite called her back to old times, this running tame of Carnforth's daughter under our roof. Nora Whitmore is my late father's widowed sister, who has stayed with us for nearly as long as I can remember. She is not so romantical as Edward but is not untainted either in that respect. She reads and praises all his stuff; she does not, to my knowledge, write it.

"I think you should return Lady Emily's visit, Chloe," she told me, with a vigorous nod of her head but without looking at me. I can hardly remember the last time she looked right at me. She is always netting, you see. It is her pride, her passion, one might almost say her life. Her blue rattan netting box is always by her side, her fingers moving with the speed and precision of long practice over her mesh. "She will never come back a fourth time if you do not return her call. It is only common courtesy to do so. We ought to have done it before now."

"She never stays home a day to receive us," I pointed out, for the visits came hard on the heels one of the other. "I have better things to do with my time."

Raising sheep is not a matter of gathering the herd once a year for clipping and sitting back and counting your money the rest of the time, as an outsider might think. It seems they are constantly being gathered — for lambing, clipping, dipping, breeding, selling, and so on. Arrangements must be made for all these matters, and of course there was the home farm to see to as well. My time was occupied pretty fully.

"It seems to me she has Edward in her eye, coming here so often. It would be a very good thing for him."

Unaware at the time of Lady Emily's dowerless state, I was inclined to agree. One had no reason to suppose Lord Carnforth's daughter would be portionless, even if the Hall was falling apart. We around the neighbourhood generally blamed its state on his advancing years and disinterest, rather than on penury.

"Perhaps you're right," I said. "We'll go tomorrow, shall we, Auntie? We'll go early and beat her coming to us."

Despite her eagerness, Aunt Nora's reply must wait till she had drawn the mesh out of her netting and inserted it to begin a new row. "Excellent," she agreed then, without lifting her eyes. "We will be able to judge by Carnforth's reaction how he feels about it. If this spate of visits has not his approval, they must stop. I cannot think Lady Emily is the sort of girl to be sneaking off behind her papa's back. He must know what she is about."

I believe Nora changed her mind when we went to the Hall. It would surprise me very much if Lord Carnforth even remembered he had a daughter, much less knew or cared what she did with her time. In short, he was three sheets to the wind when we arrived, and it was a morning call we paid.

"Who's there? Who's banging on the demmed door?" he bellowed, from some room beyond our view.

A servant wearing threadbare and spotty livery admitted us.

"His lordship is h'indisposed," he told us grandly, in that haughty manner of the aristocracy's servants. "Is it her ladyship you've come to see?"

My own first thought was to escape the place at top speed. I had never seen such filth and confusion. There was dust and dirt everywhere. The windows were gray, the hangings limp and yellowed. Sofas sagged and silver tarnished to a greenish-black ir-ridescence amidst a welter of papers and debris on table tops. There was even a pair of boots sitting on a table in the saloon. Certainly Lady Emily could not personally be expected to keep so large a place clean, but if she were any manager at all, it seemed to me she could have harried the servants into doing better than this We are not rich at Ambledown either, but there is no dust on the furnishings.

"If you please," Nora answered firmly and strode to a sofa, carefully lifting her skirts about her ankles.

Lady Emily was soon with us, smiling serenely. She looked like a beautiful pink rose that had somehow bloomed in a dust bin. Emily has hair that is nearly golden, just a shade darker, and she has blue eyes. Her colour is high, not washed out like some blondes. She happened to be wearing a pink gown, not the most felicitous colour for her complexion in my view, but reinforcing the floral likeness. She seemed totally unaware of her surroundings. "How nice of you to call," she said, beaming with pleasure. "Does Papa know you are here?"

"Your father is — indisposed, the butler tells us," I replied, feeling embarrassed for her.

"I daresay he did not sleep well last night," she said blandly. The girl was either an actress or incredibly naive. "Pray have a seat. I shall call for some tea."

We sat gingerly on a musty sofa while Lady Emily pulled vainly on a bell cord, which I am quite convinced connected to no bell anywhere. In any case, no servant ever came to bring tea, a fact that soon fell from her mind (but not, alas, from mine; I was thirsty for a cup.) It was the strangest visit I have ever endured, and I have lived through some odd ones at the homes of our local eccentrics.

Lady Emily was a charming hostess, asking for all our family and the more important domestics and discussing parish affairs, just as though her father were not bellowing out an obscene song at the top of his lungs in the next chamber. She ignored him, which I found rather difficult to do. She likewise ignored the missing tea tray, the squalor all around her, and the little hobgoblin of a man in a hideous brown jacket who darted to and fro in the saloon, making an inventory of all the rubbish.

At length, I could contain my curiosity no longer. "Is your father having an inventory made?" I asked.

"No, it is a bailiff, Miss Barwick," she told me, smiling politely. "We have the bailiffs in the house, for non-payment of bills. They will take some things that are not entailed and sell them, I believe. Do you plan to attend the assembly this month?"

"I never attend the assemblies, Lady Emily," I told her.

"I'm sure Edward would be happy to take you," she went on,

making it pretty clear why she was interested in *my* attending. "Mr. Carrick was saying only last Sunday after church that he is forever trying to coax you to attend."

I could not like to say Mr. Carrick was the reason I stayed away, but he was. Since he had bought up an estate on the other side of the mere two years before, he had taken into his head he was in love with me and hounded me so mercilessly that I avoided any occasions that would throw him in my way. "I gave all that sort of thing up a few years ago," I said vaguely, implying it was my advanced years that accounted for it, though I had not considered myself a spinster by any means when Carrick landed in town. Not quite firmly nailed to the shelf at the time — a little more firmly attached to it since then.

"Edward will hardly go alone," she added, with an artless look.

Aunt Nora unfolded a clean handkerchief and pulled out her netting, placing the woolens on the linen to prevent soiling. This uncouth act went unnoticed by our hostess. "Are you making a shawl, Mrs. Whitmore?" she asked.

Nora admitted it to be the case, then began a series of ingenious questions, each seemingly pointless by itself, which joined together to amount to a third degree of financial affairs at Carnforth Hall. Within a half hour we had learned that old Lord Carnforth was rapidly drinking himself into his grave and was virtually bankrupt, with the estate mortgaged to the hilt, Lady Emily without a penny of dowry, and the heir to it all, Cousin John Gamble, off somewhere in India, unaware surely of the way his inheritance was being sluiced down the drain.

"Should Mr. Gamble not be sent for, notified how matters stand here at home?" Nora suggested.

"Papa is convinced he would not care," was the uninterested reply.

"He has been in India for quite fifteen years now, you must know. It was thought when he went that Cousin Wilbur Gamble would inherit, as Papa has no sons, but Cousin Wilbur was drowned, and it is Uncle John's son who will come into the title." I found it significant she did not add "and estates". I suspect the latter would fall into that domain where bankrupt estates go.

"You never mean Black Jack Gamble is to be the heir?" Aunt Nora demanded, with a startled expression on her face.

"Why yes, that is what Papa called him," Emily admitted. "But he is not really a black man. It is his hair, I think…"

"Oh, well in that case, it is no difference whether the estate is lost now or later," Nora said, in a fatalistic, resigned sort of a way. She was soon winding up her woolens, stuffing them back into their blue box, and thanking Lady Emily for the visit, there having been no tea for which to render thanks.

We were off in our landaulet, back home to Ambledown. I might just take a moment to explain that this means of conveyance was less elegant than it sounds. Ours was an antique, one of the first landaulets seen in the country, so ancient that it had been imported by our ancestors from Germany before they became the fashion in England. The front half of the top had wilted into mildewed disrepair a decade or so ago, so that it was only of use on a fine summer day. One of its chief advantages was that it was capable of being pulled by one horse, whereas the old black family carriage is so heavy it requires a team to haul it. If you hope to exceed six miles an hour you would need four horses, but we are infrequently in such an almighty rush as that to get anywhere. In a fit of poetical light-heartedness a year ago, Edward painted our landaulet a rather pretty apple green colour, and I with my own fingers added a pair of yellow geometric arabesques down the sides. Nora declared at the time that it resembled nothing so much as a travelling tinker's wagon and called it by that name. Edward and I did likewise, to let our neighbours know we considered the carriage an item of family whimsey, not a serious vehicle.

As I took Belle's reins into my hands, I turned to Nora. "What did that remark about Black Jack Gamble mean, pray? How does it come *you* know something about the man, and I do not?"

"He has been gone for fifteen years, Chloe. You are not so old yet that you could have heard of his crimes before he left. Still a child you were. You must remember *seeing* Jack Gamble though. He visited the Hall a few summers before he went away. He lived over in the west district — Cumberland."

I harkened in my mind back through the mists of time to the

summers when I had been a carefree eleven or twelve. I dredged up a hazy impression of a dark-haired youth on a bay stallion, thundering across the meadow, down the road, and occasionally into town, swaggering and impressing the local bucks and damsels with his posturing. "Did he win the fell-race one year?" I asked.

Fell-racing is unique to our district, I believe. It is incredibly arduous — climbing up the fells and scampering down again. It sounds like child's play till you take into account the roughness of the terrain, the naked rock in places, the treacherous moss in others, and of course the great speed involved. No lowlander has ever won, to my knowledge. Whoever wins is the local hero for a week or so, which is perhaps how I came to remember Jack Gamble at all.

"I believe he did. Fancy your remembering that. His other exploits would not be known to a child, however."

"I am no longer a child, Auntie."

"It never ceases to amaze me how well-reared young ladies are so eager to hear tales of wrong-doing. It was not spoken of a great deal hereabouts, but Lady Carnforth was still alive at the time, and a friend of mine. She told me the story. Jack seduced his cousin Wilbur's fiancée. That same year he won the fell-race, it was. He was popular with the ladies after that, and Millie Henderson was always a ninnyhammer anyway."

"You mean he actually got her in trouble?"

"Enough trouble that Wilbur felt free to call off the match. And then Jack hadn't the integrity to offer the girl marriage but sneaked off to India and left her in the lurch. I imagine it is the only reason he ever went, for he had a decent home and prospects from his father. Nothing so grand as Carnforth Hall you know, but a respectable estate. A mine, I think his papa owned, like Carnforth. Though it might have been sheep, as he won the fell-race. It is usually won by a sheep farming family."

I regarded her with an unbelieving eye, for I knew perfectly well that Millie Henderson had been happily married to another gentleman for some years, as she would not have been had she been termed ruined.

"Old Carnforth patched up some match for her," Nora explained. "The old aristocratic families arrange these matters. In any case, Jack Gamble was never any good. He was a wild young buck — gaming, wenching, gambling, fighting, and riding. We were glad to see the back of him, I can tell you. So if *he* is to inherit Carnforth Hall, it hardly matters whether the estate goes to the courts now or a year from now. Of more importance to us is that Lady Emily hasn't a penny to her name. Edward cannot offer for her. Pity. Even if she had five thousand... But with the mortgage at home standing so high, it is not to be thought of."

As Nora's eyes were not required for netting in the carriage, she could spare me a glance, and as mine were required for driving, I could ignore it. I knew, though, that she regarded me hopefully. If I accepted Tom Carrick, of course, Edward would have one less encumbrance. Or perhaps two, if Nora came to live with Tom and me.

"I don't consider it a total tragedy," I said. "Outside of her right to the title of 'Lady', and of course a pretty face, Emily has not much to offer. She is not the best manager the countryside has seen, is she?"

"To be sure she is not, Chloe. You are, but you would continue to manage family affairs until... as you always have done."

"A new mistress might have something to say about that," I pointed out.

"Not Lady Emily. She would not care two straws for it. It really is a great pity," she repeated, then cast her gaze about the countryside, to nod and smile at the blue-gray hills in the distance, patched with green and dotted with sheep.

"At least Edward has not fallen madly in love with her," I mentioned.

"If she keeps hanging about the way she has been doing, he soon will," she forecast gloomily.

She was right. Lady Emily kept on coming, at least twice, often four times, a week throughout that spring and summer. She caught Edward at home often enough that her beauty penetrated his consciousness. He was half in love with Lady Emily and half in love with love, as becomes a poet. He was not so fond of her as to curtail his jaunts over to Rydal Mount to meet with Mr. Wordsworth's circle.

It seems to me that a man wishing to do honour to our beautiful Lake District (as our northwestern corner of England has been misnamed since the poets brought it into fashion) should do so with brush and canvas. All these poets have accomplished is to have us overrun with tourists who come in carriages to glance at what they call the lakes. Actually there is not a lake in the whole area. We natives refer to our bits of water as meres and tarns. A lake is something much larger, and much less lovely. It was Thomas Gray who first went spouting tales of the "lakes" to be enjoyed here. He was soon followed by others — Southey, Coleridge, and of course our own William Wordsworth, who lived right in Grasmere for several years.

Over the past ten years we have become *the* tourist attraction of the country. I cannot begin to describe the mess and confusion these visitors bring. In the first place, they have no real appreciation of our landscape. They peer from a carriage window when the beauty can only be gained by walking, by clambering up fells to look down at the tarns of various hues and shapes. The colour will change before your very eyes from blue to green or even black, as the clouds pass by overhead. The waters nestle in secret dales and valleys between the hills, the pikes, and the fells. The tourists who do not get out of their carriages miss the bracing air, the aroma of the bog myrtle, most of all the challenge of the fells. The fells are the real attraction of the place.

For maximum viewing pleasure one should avoid coming during the bracken season, as we call that time between late June and late September, which is exactly when the greatest number of tourists come. At that time the contours of the fells are hidden by the monotonous fern that covers them like a green blanket. The weather too is wretched — too hot most of the time, relieved only by the wettest rain in the world. It comes in blankets, in sheets, in counterpanes to saturate us. You have not been wet till you have been rained on here.

If you want to see us at our best, come in April or October. Do not come in the dead of summer, like the tourists who clutter up the hotels and inns and drive up prices. Not that you will find a lack of accommodation! We have been inundated by a sea of businessmen wishing to capitalize on the new tourist industry. Many a garish mansion has been thrown up, to clash dreadfully with the simple architecture of the countryside and to take up land needed for our livelihood. I refer, of course, to our Herdwick sheep. Unlovely, smelly, oily, white-faced, and rugged as the natives, they dot the fells year round, eking out a diet that would starve other sheep and growing a coarse, long fleece used for carpets and roughage in the Cumberland tweed.

But I have digressed into a travel brochure. Edward succumbed to Nature, in the form of Lady Emily. They walked out together; his poems found a new object of dedication. The "barren fells" and "limpid blue pools" of yore were transformed into "sweet delights" of femininity. The limpid blue pools remained but came in pairs, fringed with lashes. Edward had not begun to think of anything so down-to-earth as marriage, I am sure, but Emily was beginning to look about the saloon with a somewhat proprietary eye. She had hemmed up half a dozen handkerchiefs for him, embroidered with a crooked design which Nora thinks is supposed to be an E. I think she would be better employed wielding a mop or broom at home.

Nora had not completely abandoned all thoughts of sharing the roof with a Lady. She is a *wee* bit of a snob, to tell the truth, but no one is perfect. "A pity about the dowry," she was wont to say, but soon began adding such leading remarks as, "At least she is not demanding. She is always perfectly happy with pot luck." On another occasion the remark, in the same insinuating spirit, was, "How very much at home Emily (sans the Lady now) looks in our little tinker's wagon."

Each sally was met with a steely eye from myself. I (who was in charge of the accounts for the establishment) knew we must marry Edward to at least a small heiress, not an impecunious Lady who might well change her demands once she was installed as mistress of Ambledown. Due to Edward's detached, lackadaisical way of going on, June waned into July, the heat rose, the old earl at Carnforth Hall declined, and still there was no firm announcement of any approaching nuptials. There was soon an announcement of a much more distressing nature to plague us, but it had nothing to do with Edward or Emily or marriage.

2

AMBLEDOWN (MY HOME, if I failed to mention it) is located just at the northern tip of Lake Grasmere, right at the heart of the Lake District. Windermere, just below us, is thought to be prettier by some, but I prefer the wilder, craggier fells of home. Being right at the hub of the whole delightful region, Grasmere has fallen due to most of the unwanted tourist activity. We blame the majority of this on a certain Captain Wingdale, retired officer of the Royal Navy. His pockets are heavy with prize money taken during the late wars. It is his aim to make them even heavier by destroying our whole town and neighbourhood with his business activities. Bad enough he threw up a spurious Elizabethan inn, whose half timbers stand out like a sore thumb in this area that has still a strong Nordic flavour. Bad enough indeed that every cit and clerk who can afford the journey comes with a carriageful of children to fill his rooms and our streets, and to make such a racket into the night and on the Sabbath that the local inhabitants have no peace. Captain Wingdale is in the process of modernizing us by holding assemblies in the largest room of his hotel — not monthly, nor even weekly, but *nightly* throughout the summer for the delight of his clients and the less discriminating of the local inhabitants.

There are some folks broad-minded enough to forgive him all these atrocities, for while he has driven up prices in the local shops to ridiculous heights, he has brought more custom than usual to the village. Rooms are let by many a spinster and widow who would otherwise be deprived of this little additional income. Tea shops flourish; souvenirs are imported from London and stamped with the names of the various lakes; pamphlets abound bruiting our charms to the travellers. As Ambledown is two miles from the village, even I was large-hearted enough to forgive Wingdale, but his latest crime neither I nor anyone else for miles around can condone.

The crime (and the distressing announcement referred to earlier) is this: Captain Wingdale has taken into his head to create an entirely new town. It is to be located between the present village and Ambledown — right on our doorstep, you see. He has used the coincidence of there being several places ending in the termination "dale" to name the town after himself, Wingdale, ignoring the fact that Dunnerdale, Grizedale, and so on are not named after people, but are in fact dales — valleys. Wingdale is nothing of the sort. It will be built on a slight incline. By some underhanded means he snapped up several acres of land outside of Grasmere and was busy every day trying to seize the rest of it. It would not surprise me in the least if he has set his greedy sights on Ambledown. Indeed, the plan of his new town is incomplete without it. Our ancestral home forms the focal point of the road that runs north from Grasmere, with Barwick Pike towering behind it. Ambledown would be incorporated into the town even if Edward manages to hold on to it — a thing by no means certain in our perilous financial state. The plans for Wingdale are on prominent display in the window of Wingdale Hause. In his sublime ignorance, the Captain mistook the old Nordic "hause" to mean house, or so I assume. It means a narrow pass, in case you are interested. Wingdale Hause is his spurious Elizabethan inn, right on the main street. He pulled down three shops and the existing inn to build it. The inn was of great historical interest, being several hundred years old, but Wingdale does not even profess to have any interest in history, unless it is recent enough to concern his own naval exploits.

When you have been accustomed to look out your door or window on to quiet meadows, to serene fells and water, it is distressing to consider that within a year or two the sight will be changed to a hodge-podge of poorly designed modern cottages with not two yards of land between them, those two yards doubtlessly cluttered with noisy youngsters and dogs. He speaks, too, of bringing some "industry" in as an added incentive to lure people to Wingdale. The exact nature of the industry has not been revealed, which is in itself suspicious. If it were some clean, light business, he would not hesitate to name it. My imagination fails to give me any notion what he has in mind, but with mines close-by the ugly spectre of some smoke-belching foundry occasionally looms up.

None of us at home had a good word to say about his scheme. Neither had Emily, as soon as she learned Edward was against it. She sat with us on a Sunday afternoon out in the garden, where Nora netted (what else?) and I was ostensibly studying Edward's latest poetical effusion, with a view to criticizing it before submission to *Blackwood's Magazine*.

"I hear the Leroys have sold to Wingdale," Edward commented idly, with a glance down the road in the direction of Ronald Leroy's home.

There was only the Chapman's farm remaining between Leroy's and Ambledown. "You cannot mean it!" I exclaimed, dropping his ode to the ground in my consternation. "Why on earth would Ronald do such a thing? He is against the new town."

"He has had a terrible run of luck," Edward reminded me. "You remember how many head of sheep he lost when some poison got into his spring dip. Close to a hundred it was, and then at the end of June the wool he had stored in his barn for market was burned up. He has been scrambling to meet his mortgage ever since. It turned out Wingdale had bought it from the bank, and he foreclosed. Well, Leroy was three months overdue. Wingdale was very gentlemanly about it, they say in town. He has given Ronald a few months to relocate and has even offered to buy his herd from him so that he will have money to get started up in something else."

"Where can he go? What will he do? He doesn't know any other business but sheep," Nora lamented, when the exigencies of her work allowed her to draw breath.

"I expect he will go to work for one of the larger farmers. Not much else he *can* do. I wish I could afford to hire him," Edward said. Poor Edward. His heart was in the right place, but his head, alas, was in the clouds. He could hardly afford to hire *me*, at the price of rack and manger.

Edward looks as a poet should look, with a fine dreamy eye, a sweet expression, and an ineffectual mouth which either smiles or sulks but never assumes the determined line of a man of resolution. He looked to Emily and fell into a reverie, very likely composing a few lines on her beauty. He was not to be disturbed during these moments of creation — it was tacitly understood. I addressed my next remark to Nora.

"We'll be the next to go," I warned her. "I shall go to the bank tomorrow and make sure our mortgage has not been taken over by Wingdale. I doubt it is legal for them to sell it without letting us know."

"Wingdale is always legal," Nora pointed out. "He has hired that London solicitor full time, to represent his interests."

"I begin to wonder whether he has not hired an arsonist full time as well. You remember how he got Berkens' place last winter? A fire started in the barn and spread to the house."

"That kind of talk will get you in trouble," she cautioned me. "Wingdale's lawyer threatened Berkens with a slander suit when he suggested the fire was not accidental."

"It's not slander if you can prove it. If I were a man I would do some investigating," I said, speaking rather loudly in Edward's general direction.

I did not really hope he would hear. His next speech showed me my error. "You are thinking Beetham had something to do with it, Chloe."

"Beetham? Why should I think anything of the sort?"

"Well, Beetham used to work for Berkens, and when he left him he went to Leroy, so it might look like a connection, but he was in the tavern at Wingdale Hause the night Leroy's wool was burned, so it could not have been his doing."

"I had not realized such rumours were running around town. We'll have to be a good deal more careful, if Wingdale *is* causing these fires and accidents," I said, feeling a strong sense of alarm.

The afternoon was unpleasant enough, with the news of our old neighbour losing his farm. It soon deteriorated even further when I spotted Tom Carrick jiggling down the road in his whisky. He often comes to court me on a Sunday afternoon. The rest of the week he is busy, thank goodness. The wooing has taken on an even stronger flavour of distaste since the proposal. I would have refused him by now were it not for Nora's constant singing of his praises, and my own fears for our future.

"Why, here is *Tom!*" she said, glancing up as she stopped to turn the mesh in her netting. How she could imbue one monosyllable with so much approval is a wonder. She drew it out, in a sing-song way, going up and down in tones. The two lovers (Edward and Emily, I mean) turned warm, conspiratorial smiles on me. Soon their gaze reverted to each other. A silent agreement being reached between them, they arose to wander off towards Barwick Pike. As Emily was wearing patent slippers, I trusted they did not have in mind climbing it.

Tom dismounted and tethered the reins to a tree, then came towards me. He was carrying an ominous bundle, newspaper-wrapped, which was the manner in which he brought his edible offerings of fish and fowl, and an occasional rabbit. "Don't leave us, Nora," I said before he got within hearing range. She was unhappy, but obedient.

I really don't know why it is I cannot love Tom, or at least like him better than I do, for I am hardly in the springtime of life, where love is all to me. There is nothing amiss in either his appearance or character. He is tall enough (five feet, nine inches), handsome enough (dark hair, fair skin, not deformed in either face or body), rich enough (five thousand per annum), and old enough (thirty-three years). There is just some little *je ne sais quoi* lacking. Maybe I do *sais quoi,* but hesitate to relate it. The man is possessed of no single atom of that element whose excess I have been lamenting all these pages in my brother — romance. Like everything else, it is wanted in the proper degree, which is to say in this case, sparingly. When Tom proposed, for example, he complimented me on my good character, my hard work at keeping Ambledown running, my economy, my interest in the local charity work, and my family's old origins. He mentioned that I would be a useful helpmate to him. Not in just those words, of course, but that was the gist of it. I do not denigrate that he took account of these matters, but that it was these and no others he chose to mention at such a time. I did not expect to hear him say, as Captain Wingdale once did, that I was "the prettiest little lady in town". I am not, but I hope I am not quite an offence to the eyes either. If my brown hair would only turn black, my blue eyes green, my few freckles fade, and my chin shrink about an inch, I think I might be said to possess some claims to beauty.

Tom was upon us, making his bows and asking permission to take up the chair vacated by Edward, while he looked at his soggy newspaper and his hands and my hands, feeling, I suppose, that he should be making some more formal greeting. He is a little inclined to formality.

"Have a chair, Tom," Nora said.

"Pity about Ronald Leroy," he commented, sitting down, still holding his bundle. The sun was shining, blackbirds wheeled overhead, and I was wearing a new fichu on my best gown. The man had come courting, but his first words after being seated were, "Pity about Ronald Leroy."

"We were just discussing it," Nora answered, glancing to the newspaper expectantly.

"We were wondering whether Wingdale is not having these fires set," I said, and watched for his reaction.

"There is no evidence of that. I would not say such a thing in company, Chloe," he warned me, with a nervous look.

"He is too sharp to leave any evidence," I pressed on. "There is only Chapman's between Grasmere and Ambledown now. If Chapman's goes up in smoke, I mean to call in a constable and have it investigated. In fact, it ought to be done now. The men of the area should get together and *insist*," I said, casting a challenging look on him.

"Chapman won't give him any trouble," was his answer. "He has got the concession of brewmaster for Wingdale Hause. Well, he never had more than a nominal interest in sheep and will be glad to be rid of what he has. He is tickled pink with the new village. It will bring a good deal of prosperity to the area. I'm not sure it is a bad thing, when all's said and done."

"It is a wretched thing! You would say so too if your estate were situated in his path, instead of safely away on the far side of the mere."

"As to that, Miss Barwick, you are welcome to join me any time, away from all the construction that will soon be going forth. And your aunt, Mrs. Whitmore, as well," he added punctilious-ly, with a nod to include her in his proposal. "As to Edward," he went on, to account for the whole family, "I expect there would be plenty of room for him at Carnforth Hall. Wingdale will not plan to include *it* in his village."

Naturally we had not bruited about town the state of Carn-forth's finances, but it struck me of a sudden that the Hall might very well be included in Wingdale's ultimate plans. It would be easy picking. He might have the mortgages for it in his pocket this minute for all we knew. The Hall had sat like a fortress guarding that situation known as Kirkwell Pass for centuries. The blood fairly boiled to think of its falling to Wingdale's commer-cial hands. He would turn it into a haunted house, or some such thing, to attract customers. Ices and lemonades and gingerbread would be served on the grounds, assemblies held nightly in the ballroom. And the only people in the world to prevent this hap-pening were Lord Carnforth, bellowing out his obscene songs in a drunken stupor, and Lady Emily, mooning around under the trees with Edward.

"Someone ought to notify Mr. Gamble in India how matters stand," I said.

"From what I hear of Jack Gamble, he is more likely to throw in his lot with Wingdale than hinder him," Tom replied. Then he launched into an exposition on a new carpet he is having in-stalled on his front staircase. These improvements to the nest are inducements to attract me into it. Any lack of refinement, any desired renovation that slips my lips regarding Ambledown is quickly instituted at Tarnmere, as Tom has foolishly called his home. He did not realize the repetition of it (a tarn being a small mere). As he has had the name carved in stone over the front portal, the name sticks.

And still the sodden newspaper was being carefully held an inch above his lap. "Can I take your parcel for you, Tom?" Nora asked, not intimating by so much as a blink that she guessed it to be a gift.

"A nice pair of trout I caught early this morning," he said, handing it to her. "Small heads and good full back, which make the best eating. Not one of those bull trout I brought you last time."

The gift served a dual function. It got rid of Nora, as the trout must be taken to the kitchen, and it informed us politely he would accept an invitation to dinner. Emily had long ago stopped bringing her offerings, but it was known that she, too, would accept a Sunday invitation to dinner. We contrived a merry meal and evening, despite Tom's finding an opportunity to press me for an answer and despite Edward's not putting his question to Emily.

As our company prepared to leave, however, it struck me that things would not long be running on in this smooth path. Tom must be given an answer; Emily must be asked the question, and either I must say yes, or she must say no. One member of the family must keep his (i.e. her) head screwed on straight. There was not much likelihood of Edward's doing so.

"I have made good headway this evening," Nora said, stuffing her woolens away and arising to shake out her skirts. "Two full inches done."

"What are you making now, Aunt Nora?"

"A wedding gift," she said archly, and smiled. Her mind had been running in the same groove as my own. She had got farther in her reckonings than I. I believe that coy smile meant she planned to attend two weddings in the near future.

3

THE ANNOUNCEMENT OF Wingdale's new town had already thrown us into one conniption. While we were still wrestling with it, another major change occurred in our lives. It proved more vexatious than Wingdale (the town), though it was greeted at first with a sense of relief. Jack Gamble returned from India to take over control of Carnforth Hall. We learned it before anyone else by virtue of Emily's habit of popping over to see us at all hours of the day. To do the girl justice, I must state at once that she did not usually land in on us before breakfast, which we take at half past eight. On that uncomfortably warm summer day, she did just that.

She was standing at the foot of the stairs when I descended that morning. I knew from the staring look in her eyes that something untoward had happened and thought it must be her father's death — a thing that was awaited, expected at any time. Not that he had taken any turn for the worse, but he was old and ailing. There was a lost, vulnerable look on her pretty little face. It flashed into my head at once that now Edward must marry her. She could not go on staying alone in that ramshackle old house, with bailiffs for company. It was unfortunate from a financial point of view, but it would surely happen, and I would accept it. On an impulse I opened my arms to her, for she looked so helpless.

She flung herself into them gratefully and hugged me. Starved for human affection, I thought. I never felt so kindly towards her before — or since for that matter. "Oh, Miss Barwick, he has come back!" she declared, when we released our hold on each other.

With the notion in my head that her papa was dead, I pictured a ghost hovering at her shoulder. Her next speech disabused me of the idea. "Jack Gamble has returned from India. Someone sent for him — some judge or something, because of Papa's condition you know. He looks for all the world like an Indian, and talks so strangely. I am frightened of him."

"Oh, is *that* all? I feared your father was dead."

"No, he is very angry, but he is not dead. He says he will throw Jack out again, as the family did before, but Jack says if he does he'll have a magistrate down to assess the estate, for it has been let go shockingly, and as he is the heir he has the legal right to do so. He is the most wicked man I ever met—so rude to Papa!"

"He has no good reputation," I agreed mildly, wondering what it was best to do.

"I *cannot* stay in the house with him," was her next speech, accompanied by a pleading glance from her big, moist eyes and a tremble of her lower lip.

"My dear, with your father there, there is no danger."

"Papa is never sober for two hours a day. And the way Cousin Jack looks at me. I am so frightened, Miss Barwick."

It was an unforeseen complication, indeed, that Gamble might decide to seduce his little cousin. "Come and have some coffee. We'll talk it over with Aunt Nora and Edward," I parried, to give myself time to think.

She read some promise into this that we would protect her. She relaxed noticeably, a smile spreading across her face and her eyes sparkling with pure excitement. She was more vivacious that morning than I had ever seen her, full of stories of her cousin, who was a walking piece of wickedness from her account.

"He arrived at midnight, Miss Barwick! Was there ever such an example of bad manners? Papa was not feeling well, and *I* was hauled out of bed by the servants — at his orders — to welcome him. He was so insulting, looking about at the house with great distaste and always speaking of money, in the most ill-bred fashion. He asked me if I had a beau, and how much money *he* had, for I thought it safer to mention Edward in case Cousin Jack should get ideas about me. He said I was outrageously pretty, you see, and looked at me in such a way, as though he were looking right through me with his horrid black eyes.''

"He didn't touch you — molest you?" I asked sharply.

"I don't think so. That is — he kissed me, but only on the cheek."

"What does he look like?"

"Like a heathen. He has skin as brown as tanned leather. He wears English clothing, however. A rather nice blue jacket, which he got in London before coming here. He says he has some trunks coming with presents for me. I won't accept them."

"What sorts of presents?" I asked, wondering that she would reject them sight unseen.

"Muslin and some statues — I don't know what all. He hates Captain Wingdale's new inn, and threatened to set fire to it. Imagine! He is really shocking," she concluded, saucer-eyed at such outrageous behaviour. Some secret corner of my heart went out to the man, as he shared my aversion to Wingdale's architectural monstrosity.

The story was repeated with a few embellishments and a few deletions (most noticeably the kiss on the cheek) when Nora and Edward joined us. I felt this ought to be told to them, and did so, as she was a little shy.

"That settles it then. You must stay here, my dear," Edward told her.

The three of us looked at him, assuming some roundabout hint of a wedding might be mentioned. Nora and I undertook to give him privacy, each finding an excuse to carry her coffee cup away from the table, but in a quarter of an hour they joined us in the morning parlour, with no mention of any offer having been made.

"I am taking Emily home in the tinker's wagon. She will pack up her bags and come to spend a while with us, Chloe," he said.

I was half relieved, for my first wave of pity for the girl had subsided, and I was again thinking how fine it would be if it were Edward who could be our salvation through a good marriage and not myself. Surely if he loved her he would have offered now.

After they left, Nora made a delightful suggestion. "This

cousin might give the girl some dowry, to be rid of her," she said. "The lads often return quite rich from India. If he is one of those Nabobs, he might spare her a few thousand pounds."

"That would be better luck than we are accustomed to," I said hopefully.

"If he himself is planning to marry, for example, he would be glad to see her settled. Edward must marry her now, don't you think?"

"Something must be done. She cannot be expected to live in that hovel with a rake and a drunken father. Neither can she be expected to move in here bag and baggage without a betrothal at least."

When they returned from the Hall with two straw suitcases, however, she seemed prepared to do just that. I showed her to a guest room, leaving her to unpack her own belongings, for we were not overly supplied with help at the time.

I was curious to get a look at Jack Gamble. To this end, Nora and I piled into the tinker's wagon and drove into the village, passing Leroy's place along the way. The servants were taking curtains down from the windows already. The view struck a positive blow to my heart. Wingdale had men out surveying the land, sticking red-tipped sticks into the ground at certain spots. Awash with curiosity, I asked their chief what he was about.

"We're laying out the new street, Miss," he answered cheerfully. "The Captain's going to straighten her out. 'Make a road straight as an arrow, lads', he ordered us. These old crinkum-crankum paths are wasteful."

"Gee-up, Belle," I urged our mare, in an effort to refrain from blistering the man with my tongue. Straighten out the road indeed! This charming road that had been set out centuries before, to give a traveller the best views of our fells and dales and tarns. The man was a monster! Next he would be razing the mountains to the ground to give us a nice flat plain, all in the name of economy and modernization.

We saw nothing of Jack Gamble in the village. His arrival was known, discussed, conjectured upon wildly, but no one had seen him yet. Nora purchased some moss green netting materials, and

I a marmalade pot to replace one broken recently at home. What was lost had been of Waterford crystal, beautifully shaped. What took its place was a plain white porcelain, at six shillings and tuppence. It was indicative of our falling fortunes. I wager Wingdale had Waterford crystal on his table.

It was a frustrating, unsatisfactory day from all points of view. The evening was perfectly wretched. Edward was off to a poetry meeting at Rydal Mount. As soon as he left Emily found herself too tired to sit with Nora and me, but went to her room to sulk. "Maybe I should go home," she said on her way out the door, to punish us for Edward's defection. "They must be wondering where I am, in any event."

"Did you not tell them?" I asked, dumbfounded.

"I told Cook," she called back over her saucy, flouncing shoulder.

Anyone but a yahoo must realize we could not virtually abduct the daughter of Carnforth Hall without there being some repercussions. While I debated with Nora the relative niceties of asking Emily to write or of writing to her father myself, the front knocker pounded. There was some peremptory quality in the sound that intimated the knocker was no servant, but an angry gentleman. I was virtually certain it would be Jack Gamble.

I knew from Emily more or less how he would look, but being accustomed to such tame men about the house as Edward and Tom, nothing had prepared me for my first sight of him. The instant he strode into the saloon the air seemed to crackle as though he emanated an electrical charge, like the ebony bars Edward used to rub with cat fur and apply to pith balls when he was a boy scientist. Mr. Gamble was as black as those ebony bars, too. Black hair, black eyes, black jacket, skin not a whole lot lighter. He filled the doorway and gave the impression a moment later of filling the room, though he was not one of those enormous, barrel-chested men. He was tall, broad-shouldered, tapering to a trim waist.

"Good evening," he said grimly, glancing around with a lively but careless interest, hardly letting his eyes linger longer on Nora and myself than on the well-worn sofa. "One of you is Miss Barwick, I assume?" His voice was loud, buzzing with arrogance.

"I am Miss Barwick," I admitted, rather wishing I were not.

"I'm Jack Gamble."

"I am happy to make your acquaintance."

"Charmed," he allowed, in a bored voice.

"This is my aunt, Mrs. Whitmore."

"Charmed again."

"Won't you have a seat, Mr. Gamble," I suggested. My heart was hammering with excitement and guilt, after having just learned of Emily's manner of leaving home. My voice came out firm enough, however. If he said charmed once more, I meant to jump up and show him out the charming door, guilty or no.

"Thank you. I have come to see Mr. Barwick. Is he in?" He sat down with a haughty posture, head and shoulders back, and crossed one leg over the other.

"No, sir, he is out this evening."

"When will he be back?"

"Late, but if you have some business to discuss, *I* run Ambledown," I said, knowing the business at hand was Emily.

"Indeed! Extraordinary," he said, his dark brows rising an inch while he regarded me with amusement, in the spirit of one admitting to a lowering curiosity in a blue dog or a flying pig. "Is that done nowadays, for *women* to run an estate?"

"I have just told you it is done here, Mr. Gamble."

"Quite, but is it done anywhere else?"

"No, I am unique in that respect," I answered, piqued at his derision. "Have you come about Emily?"

"I am here to take her home," he answered, trying to make it sound as though she had been passing a social evening with us, no more.

Nora, the coward, said she would go upstairs and tell Emily he had come. Such was the effect he had on people. Nora had been the most insistent all day that Emily *must* stay with us for the meanwhile. What I had seen of the man thus far, including his bold eyes that examined a lady far too closely, did not incline me to change our plan. Quite the contrary, one cringed to think of that poor girl in a house with him, unprotected by any reliable chaperone.

"Emily wishes to remain with us for the time being. She left word with the servants to that effect, I believe," I told him, wishing she had left word with her father.

"It is more customary for a lady to leave word with the *family* when she plans an extended visit, ma'am. Her father is not aware of her plans."

"Nor of anything else at this hour of the night, I fancy."

He looked startled at my plain speaking. He had heard nothing yet. I would, if necessary, put my feelings into Anglo-Saxon that no one could pretend to misunderstand.

"Does Lady Emily come here often?" he asked.

"Very frequently. Hardly a day passes that we do not see her."

"To spend the *night* in a bachelor's house, I mean."

"No, sir, this is the first time."

"Is there a particular reason for it?"

I was becoming annoyed with his probing eyes. I stared back at him, assuming the boldest countenance I could to match his own. "You would know more about that than I. She expressed the wish *not* to stay at home at this time. We invited her to join us."

"We'll see what she has to say for herself," he decreed, then leaned back, crossed his arms, and said not another word till Nora re-entered the room. This was not done in thirty seconds, nor even in three minutes. It was a long time the two of us sat, silent as stuffed owls — he staring around the room, I following his eyes till I became bored with it. Then I took up a ladies' magazine and flipped through it, showing him I could be as rude as he, despite having had no opportunity of learning international bad manners outside the country.

"Emily has the headache," Nora said in a timid, apologetic way as soon as she came back.

"Let me get this quite clear," Gamble said, uncrossing first his arms, then his legs to allow him to lean forward in what he thought was an intimidating manner, with one hand on a hip, the other on his knee. "Am I to understand you have encouraged

27

the girl to run away from her home because of my *presence* in it?"

Nora began making tch'ing noises in her throat from sheer nerves. I would about as lief have faced the Spanish Inquisition as that glowering face, but I regarded him coldly.

"No, sir, you are mistaken in thinking she needed any encouragement. It was entirely her own idea."

He accepted this home truth without so much as a frown or glower. "The gudgeon," he said angrily. He stood up abruptly. I looked fearfully to the stairway, wondering how to bar his ascent. There was not a doubt in my mind that he meant to go up and fetch her down by force. "I shall be back for her tomorrow afternoon. Pray ask her to have her things packed."

"No, I can't do that," I said.

He cocked a quizzical eye at me. "Meaning?"

"I would feel morally culpable to send her back, under the circumstances."

"You will find yourself *legally* culpable if you disobey her father's orders," he retaliated pretty sharply. "If it is my dangerous presence that sends her fleeing for safety, I shall take up residence at an inn till a chaperone can be found."

"I expect you would be perfectly comfortable at Wingdale Hause," I suggested.

"Is that the half-timbered monstrosity I saw last night on the main street of town?"

"That's it."

That earned me the blackest scowl yet. "Good evening, ma'am; Mrs. Whitmore," he said in a tight voice before stomping to the doorway. He stopped and looked over his shoulder back into the room where the two of us were staring after him, haggard from the visit. At least I don't imagine I bore up under it any better than Nora, whose face was the colour of ash. "Nice to be back home," he said in accents of heavy irony; then he stalked out.

"Do you know, Nora, I don't think Mr. Gamble will be giving Emily any dowry," I prophecied, then laughed one of those giddy, overcome-with-emotion laughs that erupts at wakes and funerals and other awful, inappropriate occasions.

28

"Lud, she'll be lucky if he doesn't give her a thrashing," she agreed. "It *does* look bad for him, her darting off as she did."

"He should not have frightened her to death then, should he? I must own I would not suggest she return, now that I have met him."

"Good gracious no. I would as soon trust a fox with a chicken. I don't know how you had the nerve to stand up to him. Edward will have to marry her now."

Edward seemed like slim protection from Jack Gamble, but I was too tired to argue. Emily came slipping down to make sure he was gone, then went back up to her room. I waited up till nearly midnight for Edward to come home. Nora retired an hour earlier. I told him of the visit, asking, "What do you plan to do about the situation?"

You are aware by now it was not my hope to urge this particular match on him, but I did mention it obliquely. His response surprised me. "We are in no position to marry at this time, Chloe."

"She doesn't eat much. That would be the only additional expense," I told him.

"No, there would be children eventually, and they cost something," he pointed out, with a rare streak of practicality. His true and utterly selfish reason for postponing the day was soon coming out. "Besides, a group of us from the Poetic Society are planning a tour of the Lake District on foot. We plan to spend a month, beginning at Grasmere in a week's time and going straight up north to Ullswater, then down counter-clockwise in a circle, with a jog down to Furness Abbey, coming home up the east side of Windermere. It will be a wonderful experience."

"You won't go in the bracken season. Surely you'll wait till October!"

"We can't wait, Chloe. Harrison has a post starting the end of August, and Fergie will be going back to university. We must go now. It is not the best time for it, but it is the only time we are all free. Six of us plan to go. You'll get my things ready, won't you, Chloe? Pack a knapsack with clean linen and mint cakes and all that, and see if we can spare a little money. Wordsworth suggests strongly we make a stop at Penrith. He used to live there, you know. He says it is beautiful.''

"What about Emily?'' I asked, overcome once again at his innate selfishness.

"The chaperone Gamble spoke of should be installed in a week's time. We aren't leaving for a week. She can stay here till then.''

"You would not be so sure about that if you had seen Gamble.''

"I *did* see him. He was in the village when I was on my way home, going into Wingdale Hause. Someone said it was Jack Gamble at least. A great, tall, dark fellow. No wonder Emily is frightened of him. I was myself.''

This speech left me in no doubt whatsoever as to who was to protect Lady Emily from her cousin. Me! This settled the matter to Edward's complete satisfaction. "Goodnight, Chloe. You won't forget to see about the money, will you? I shan't need much.''

As the slim funds we possessed all belonged to Edward by rights, this was by no means an imposition. In fact, he was generous as well as selfish: generous with money, about which he cared not a hoot; selfish with his time, which he preferred to dedicate to his Muse.

4

IN THE MORNING Emily donned my walking shoes and went for a long walk around the head of the lake with Edward, seizing what she could of his company before his departure. They took a luncheon, which outing promised to be romantic enough to precipitate the proposal. I half wished her luck, that we would have a legitimate excuse to keep her with us. She wore a suspiciously sulky face upon their return, and when I put a hint to Edward he said only, "Nothing definite is settled, Chloe. I am happy you wish for it though. I thought, a while back, you were not in favour of it."

"It is time to drink or pass the cup," I advised him.

"I am very fond of Emily," he said, in his dreamy, irresolute way, then heaved a deep sigh designed to inform a listener he was too weary to continue the discussion. I took it as a tentative suggestion of a proposal in the near future.

When Gamble came rattling the front door again that afternoon, the future was speeded up. I imagine Nora spotted his mount coming up the driveway. She arose from her chair with an unaccustomed haste, muttering "dinner" as she darted towards the kitchen. As Nora usually expresses the same interest in dinner as Edward in money, I knew it was but an excuse. I had not yet twigged to her reason for leaving. At least I had Edward for protection. Odd that one should feel the need for protection from a supposedly civilized neighbour, but I own I was grateful I had not to meet Gamble alone. The cause of all the furore, Emily, was resting abovestairs after the exertion of the picnic.

Gamble hardly bothered to glance at me. He turned the full

glare of his black orbs on poor Edward, who smiled back calmly enough. That poetic soul of his acted as an insulation against the realities of life to an alarming degree. I made introductions. Edward offered his hand in friendship. Gamble nearly pulled it from its wrist. I had to smile to myself to see my brother flex his fingers, not without pain, after the performance.

"Would you be kind enough to tell my cousin I am here to take her home," was our caller's first speech after the introductions.

"Emily is staying with us," Edward answered mildly.

"I beg to differ. Her aunt Crawford is visiting at the Hall, and she is required at home."

This aunt referred to was Mrs. Henrietta Crawford, known to her friends as Hennie. She was Lady Carnforth's married (and widowed) sister. He had chosen the closest relative to get Emily back home with no loss of time. Hennie lived no farther away than Windermere. She was a perfectly respectable woman of whom no worse ill was ever spoken but that she was the greatest skint alive. She would have chaperoned the Dragoons if it allowed her to live without expense for a few weeks. With the chaperone provided, I had run out of excuses to keep Emily with us.

Undaunted, Edward said, "I have promised her she may stay here. I cannot break my word."

I don't know what sort of promise the minx had extracted from him on that picnic, but the understanding had definitely been that she only stay till a chaperone had been installed. Gamble cast a look on him that was not even angry, only impatient. "Please get her. *Now*," he said. The air was crackling again, charged with some suppressed menace.

I looked to Edward. He looked uncertain. "I'll tell her," I said and bolted from the room, feeling very much as Nora had felt the night before, no doubt.

Emily smiled quite contentedly when I took the news up to her. "Is Aunt Hennie at the Hall? How nice! I think I should go and see her. I shan't be afraid now, with *her* there."

An unworthy wave of relief rolled over me. I went back belowstairs to hear Gamble putting the blocks to Edward. "May I know how you would propose to support her?" he demanded in

a hatefully toplofty tone. Had Edward finally made up his mind then, and spoken of a definite attachment?

As my brother uttered no reply to the question, I stepped into the breach. "Emily will be down shortly. She had decided to go home and see her aunt, Edward," I told him in a voice full of indifference.

Not to be put off with this news, Gamble continued staring at my brother. "I repeat, I doubt very much that you are able to support her in the manner to which she is accustomed." A scathing flicker of his eyes darted about our saloon, then returned to their prime target.

And still Edward, the clunch, stood with his tongue between his teeth. It was not to be borne. "I hope not indeed, sir," I shot back angrily, "for what she is accustomed to is living in pretentious squalor. I cannot think it has added much to her comfort to have a bailiff underfoot either." It is really quite horrid, being an older sister. Nature's impulses are all reversed, with the female having to protect the male (and looking a perfect shrew into the bargain. Not that I cared what our guest thought of me personally.)

"How tedious life in Grasmere has become if malicious gossip is the chief pastime. Tell me, Miss Barwick, would my cousin share the mistress-ship of the house with yourself?"

"Yes."

"How delightful for her," he said ironically.

"We rub along very well together I assure you."

"I have heard from her father that Emily has the disposition of a saint. He did not mention any tendency to martyrdom."

As the gloves were now off, I did not hesitate a minute to reply, "We all know well enough Lord Carnforth is never perfectly aware of what passes in the world."

"I should think not indeed, if he has given this misalliance his sanction. Odd he did not mention it."

"Nothing is settled. It is just an idea . . ." Edward began in a placating way. He had no sensitivity for handling people. A firm line was the only way with the likes of Gamble. Already I knew that much about the man. If you give a bully any notion of weakness, he will only press the point harder.

Emily came tripping lightly into the middle of the battlefield, to make her curtsey to her cousin. I must say she showed him a very charming smile, for a young lady who had done nothing but complain for the past twenty-four hours and more. "Is Aunt Hennie really at home?" she asked, a breathless quality in her voice showing her excitement. Her colour, perhaps, was a little high as well.

"Certainly she is, my dear," he answered in a voice as soft as velvet. Even those flashing black eyes had softened. The crackle was gone from the air. There was some tenderness in Gamble's regard as he smiled at Emily. It was difficult to see why she had ever been frightened of him, unless he was acting for our, or her, benefit. I shall admit the full depths of my own suspicious nature and state at once I also wondered whether *she* had not exaggerated the affair out of all proportion to push Edward into a firm offer.

"When did she come?" Emily asked.

"I went to Windermere and fetched her this afternoon. You were a very naughty girl, you know, to go slipping out of the house without telling us. Your father and I were worried about you." He wagged his finger at her playfully. She blushed a shade pinker and smiled up through her lashes at him. If she was not that minute trying to incite Edward into a fit of jet black jealousy, I would have been much surprised.

"I'm sorry, Cousin," she said.

Edward looked from one to the other of them in confusion. I would have given an ear to know what tales she had been telling him of her cousin. Really it was enough to make one wonder what she was up to. A few more teasing remarks passed between the two of them, while I stood watching, my stomach turning with disgust. Yet one could not but notice the striking picture they made, the fair young beauty and the tall, dark, dangerous-looking man.

"We're off then," Gamble said suddenly, arising.

"My bags aren't packed," Emily told him, and laughed.

"We'll have them sent for tomorrow," he answered, so eager to get her away that she would be going to bed in her petticoat. It was noticed as well that the things would be sent for, not even picked up in person. One would think we were running an inn.

I suppose the minor point must be conceded that Mr. Gamble had some latent, under-developed notions of propriety. He turned and thanked us for having entertained Emily before leaving, which is more than the hussy herself bothered to do. Neither of them made any mention of calling on us, or invited us to visit them.

"What do you make of that performance?" I asked Edward, after they had gone.

"He didn't seem so bad. I cannot imagine why Emily was so frightened of him."

"Frightened? Bah, she's no more frightened of him than I am, the hussy. Have you proposed to her at last?"

"Oh no. He asked me what my intentions were, you know, and that is how he came to be asking how I would support her, but I did not commit myself "

Nora, having observed their exit from the top of the stairs, came tripping in to hear what we could add in the way of visual details. She allowed it to be "odd", and with a little encouragement "very odd indeed". Edward hunched his shoulders and went out to look at the moon. He was creating an epic on a vestal virgin which I had thought referred to Emily, but it turned out to be the moon instead.

The only soul in the neighbourhood who shared my sense of pique at the treatment we received from them was Tom Carrick, when he came calling the next morning, and it was only Gamble he would allow to be at grievous fault. "You don't want anything to do with them," he said in his righteous way. "There's bad blood in the family, always was, always will be. The old lord drinks like a fish. Gamble is a confirmed libertine, and the gel sounds little better than a flirt, when all's said and done. They will deal well together."

"What — do you think he is interested in her in a romantic way?"

"Probably. He will inherit it all one of these days. The old lord will push for a match. The best thing for all concerned."

5

FOR FORTY-EIGHT HOURS we heard nothing further of Lady Emily. I ascertained while at the bank getting some money for Edward that our mortgage had not been taken over by Wingdale. Captain Wingdale had some men installing a gaudy, ugly set of arms on a hanging sign outside his inn. It looked familiar. I shall see if I can discover whose arms he has borrowed, for I doubt the Wingdales possess any. Edward kept us hopping at home preparing the linens and ninety-nine other items required for a walking trip of a month's duration. His companions in the walk came out one evening to discuss the enterprise, but ended up boring Nora and myself to yawns with their poetic foolishness. Each had to recite his latest creation, you know, all sounding very much like each other, and like bad Wordsworth. Nora at least got three inches of netting accomplished; I got nothing but a slight headache from worrying about what was transpiring at the Hall. Tom's remark had worried me. Emily was a bit of a rogue, but not rogue enough to deserve a libertine like Gamble.

After the company left, I said to Edward, "Don't you think you should go up to the Hall and see if Emily is all right?"

"She is fine. Fergie mentioned seeing her in the village — in high spirits he said. I shall go to say goodbye, however, before I leave."

Departure was still three days away. By dint of frequent repetition, I got a promise from him to go the next day. In the interim, we were not completely bereft of news from that quarter, for anyone who dropped by had a fresh rumour.

"They do say he's brought a troupe of foreigners home with

him," the higgler confided, his eyes round with interest. "Come in on the stage they did, wearing sheets and diapers. The women got strange marks on their foreheads, and the men folks, some of 'em, got whiskers and beards like bishops."

As if this were not rumour enough to keep us lively, Tom Carrick, never tardy in finding an excuse to drop by, told us somewhat more grammatically that he could vouch for it personally that both a tiger and an elephant had been smuggled through the village under cover of darkness, the former in a cage made of tree branches, the latter on foot with a native sitting on his head. It was Mrs. Partridge who had seen the parade. One would have to go through the village invisible to evade her eyes. She never sleeps, and never misses a trick. As we were on the main road to the Hall, we could see for ourselves the train of wagons wending their way up the twisting path, stocked with intriguingly closed cartons as big as carriages. One could only imagine their contents. What on earth could be in them? There were enough to furnish the Hall from the bottom floor up.

Edward was virtually useless as a spy. He went to see Emily, and returned home satisfied that the girl was not being abused in any way. He hadn't but one detail of the cargo from India. "Gamble has given her a monkey, so she will be well amused till my return."

"It sounds as though he is setting up a menagerie," Nora declared, "what with tigers and elephants and monkeys."

"The strangest creatures in it will be the human beings," Edward then remembered to mention. "I cannot imagine why he brought home so many natives. I think they are servants. They are all washing and polishing the Hall, in any case."

"Aye, *natives* is it?" Nora asked knowingly. "Half native and half Gamble is more like it."

"They do look rather like Gamble," Edward thought, with no trace of condemnation. "But then he is so dark that the likeness may be only one of complexion. In any case, Emily is happy as a dove. She has got her own woman now, a servant girl called Mulla, to take care of her. Oh, and Gamble has paid off the bailiff, Emily said."

"When is she coming to see us?" I asked, hoping for a more detailed account from her than I was apt to pry out of Edward. "She has not been here for some time now."

"She will come before I leave," he said, rooting on the table for his copy of Wordsworth, which was not usually so far away from him.

She didn't, but as it happened, she finally rambled down the afternoon of the day Edward set out for his tour. He left at daybreak. Emily came in the afternoon. She had Hennie Crawford with her, a lady known to us from former visits during the better days at the Hall. Gamble did not accompany them. The change in Emily was quite simply remarkable. What was first noticed was her more elegant toilette — a new white shawl was around her shoulders, while her curls were brushed carefully into a pannier do, gathered up from her face to hang in a basket of curls at the back. Her more demure behaviour was in all likelihood due to the presence of Mrs. Crawford. The woman was not precisely a dragon, but she had been known to complain that a card of condolence had a spelling error in it, which gives you, I trust, some notion that she was what is commonly termed a high stickler. It was the dead heat of summer, which did not deter Mrs. Crawford from wearing black mittens to match her black scowl. She had been eating onions.

We were given to understand in short order that a greater honour than we deserved had been bestowed on us in her coming. "Has Mr. Barwick left yet?" she asked eagerly. The closest thing to a smile that decorated her face during the whole visit broke out when the answer in the affirmative was given. Emily showed some traces of regret, but the Tartar was delighted.

"Did he not tell you he was to leave *early* this morning?" I asked Emily, for the day and hour of his departure had been known for a week.

"Yes, he did," she admitted. "I had hoped to come yesterday, but Aunt Hennie had the migraine, and of course it would not do for me to run about the countryside unchaperoned."

That she had been doing just that for the past several years caused not so much as a blush to stain her cheeks, the hoyden.

"Certainly not," Mrs. Crawford seconded her. "Cousin John would be highly displeased with such unladylike conduct."

"We would have been happy to fetch you, Emily, if you had let us know," I said, with a withering glance which I hope gave the duenna the idea we were not fooled by imaginary migraines.

"You *do* keep a carriage, do you?" the brazen woman asked, as though to imply we were of that class that walked through the dust to pay our calls on foot.

"Yes, ma'am, we do, and *both* of them happened to be sitting idle yesterday," I retaliated.

"As it happened, we were extremely busy all day yesterday with Mr. Gamble's cartons arriving from India," was her next sally.

I expect a little of my interest peeped out at this speech. Nora and I had been conjecturing wildly on this score for several hours.

"Artworks," she explained briefly. "Statues, gems, ancient Indian manuscripts. He has brought many scholars back with him, to be employed at the museums and universities."

"Meanwhile Edward tells me they are trying to clean up the Hall," I replied. "How are the tiger and elephant? I do hope they have not made a muddle of the artworks and manuscripts."

"Many botanical and zoological specimens of all sorts were brought back, to be studied and examined. They will be happy to receive them in London," she said with a blighting stare.

"Exeter Exchange do you mean?" I asked, "to be added to the menagerie there?"

"John brought me a monkey," Emily said brightly, having at last found an item of interest that did not appear to have been disqualified by the Tartar.

"How many scholars did he bring?" Nora asked. She wished to be polite but was bursting with curiosity, like myself.

"A dozen or so," Hennie answered. "No doubt vulgar gossip has exaggerated the whole business. I see Grasmere is no different from Windermere. The town whispering about the lord of the village."

"There is of course some talk about Lord Carnforth, due to his — illness," I answered in a sweet tone.

She bridled up like an angry mare, sparks shooting from her

cabbage-green eyes. "I was referring to Cousin John," she said.

"You cannot mean to tell me Lord Carnforth has passed away, and we not hearing a word about it!"

"Certainly not. Gossiping about their *betters* is what I meant, Miss Barwick. John will soon be the lord of the village," she explained patiently.

I opened my mouth to agree that we gossiped about not only our betters but the inhabitants of Carnforth Hall as well, but Nora got in before me. "How is Lord Carnforth?" she asked, in a conciliating spirit. I was left to read her injunction against further rudeness from the manner in which she snapped the mesh out of her netting.

We listened to an outpouring of imaginary ailments besetting the earl, of which overdrinking made up no part, for ten minutes, at the end of which time I had got my temper under control sufficiently to offer our guests a cup of tea. I could hardly believe my ears when the creature *refused!* Why on earth had she bothered to pay this call, if only to insult us?

I did not press her a second time. She did not invite us to call on them at the Hall, nor did I intimate that any second call from Mrs. Crawford would be a joy to us. Throughout the last tense minutes of the call Emily sat like a wind-up doll, receiving and obeying instructions passed silently from her aunt's green eyes. When the black-mittened hands reached for the reticule, Emily arose and began what was obviously a rehearsed speech.

"It was pleasant chatting with you again, Miss Barwick," with a little duck of the head and a chilly smile that included Aunt Nora. "No doubt we shall meet again."

"Unless Mrs. Crawford plans on taking you away from the district entirely, I expect we shall meet again in the village, Emily," I replied, every jot as civilly, for I would not give the pair of them the satisfaction of knowing I was furious.

"Cousin John *does* plan to take Emily to London to visit relatives, but not in the immediate future," the Tartar answered, with a smile of triumphant spite, and a stronger than ever whiff of onions as she opened her lips to bid us adieu.

Then they were gone, leaving Aunt Nora and me to regard

each other in offended confusion. "Not even a cup of tea would she take!" Nora exclaimed, when she had recovered speech. "I cannot think what she is about. The Barwicks are every bit as good as the Gambles — an older family if it comes to that. Our ancestor, Chloe, sat in Parliament *long* before that woman's ancestors knew who they were. Just because the nap is off our carpets doesn't mean we are nobody! To refuse a cup of tea in such a pointed way!"

"I believe that was what is known as a farewell visit, Auntie. And good riddance too. The onion-breathing dragon was serving us notice we are to cast out no further lures to Miss Two-Face to join us here at Ambledown."

"I am surprised Emily would take it so meekly, after the amount of friendship that has been between us lately."

"You forget she has been given a monkey to replace us. We cannot hope to compete with such a lively companion. This is all Gamble's doings, of course."

"I had that impression."

"Let him take her to London. The sooner the better. I don't care if we never see her two faces again."

"Poor Edward, he will take this hard," she sighed dismally.

I doubt very much he had thought of her since his departure. "I suppose Gamble thinks to nab a title for her, taking her to London for a Season. He'll have to dig into his pockets to provide a dowry, if that is his aim."

"He must be well to grass, bringing back so many things from India. The shipping fees alone would amount to something. Mrs. Partridge will know what he is worth. The banker has a set of rooms on her second story. I shall drop by next time I am in Grasmere."

6

THE RUMOURS OF strange doings at the Hall continued, as did the caravans bearing oriental splendours for Carnforth Hall. Mrs. Partridge rolled her eyes, gasped, and admitted that fifty thousand pounds had been transferred from a London bank to Gamble's local account. She would not venture a guess as to what portion stayed in London, but clearly he was a Nabob — and not a chicken Nabob either. Of the Nabob himself and his women we saw nothing till church on Sunday. We always had the black carriage dusted off for church, considering our yellow tinker's wagon to be of insufficient grandeur and excessive frivolity for this ecclesiastical occasion. The neo-Indians came in Carnforth's old rig, not so much grander than our own, though I must own the pair of grays hitched to it took the shine out of Dobbin and Belle. They were not Carnforth's team, but obviously belonged to Gamble.

Emily had been redone from head to toe, stuck into a fashionable gown that was surely from London, in a shade of blue that was nearly white, just tinted, like ice. It was simply but elegantly designed, showing her figure off to better advantage than her muslin round gowns had ever done. All the accoutrements were of the finest — blue kid slippers, blue gloves, a dainty bonnet with two short curly ostrich feathers that bent forward and tickled her left cheek. Really she looked inordinately elegant and beautiful, as though she no longer belonged here in Grasmere but was ready to take London by storm. I could not imagine who had made such a chic gown for her. Certainly not our local modiste, Miss Brown, who has exactly four designs in her repertoire. Gamble stood like a bridegroom by her side, smiling, solicitous to find the page for her in her book.

There, in church, was where the man's full plan hit me in the face. Jack Gamble planned to marry Emily. Tom Carrick, for once, was right. That was why she was being weaned away from Edward and such low company as Nora and myself. That was why the onion-eating chaperone had been installed, to protect Emily and John from any hint of scandal. The gifts of monkeys and gowns were all to allay her hatred and fear of him, to pave the way for her accepting him as a husband. I was a little surprised at his choice. I had thought Black Jack Gamble would select a more dashing female, but there — what lady of good reputation would have him? He was planning to set up as a reformed character — who would have thought to see him in church, for instance? — and was using his little cousin to lend him respectability. The revelation took my breath away. I had thought he only wanted to break off her infatuation with Edward for social and financial reasons. When the congregation stood up for the hymn I was slow to join them, and when they sat down I remained standing in a daze, till Nora gave my skirt a tug. At that point I looked around to see I stood above the throng, with half the crowd tittering at my foolishness and the other half politely pretending not to notice that Lady Emily, despite her fine feathers, was amongst the titterers, till she received a black-mittened poke in the ribs.

My aversion to Gamble was reaching a pitch that was positively un-Christian. It soared a little higher when the person selected for honour by the Nabob after the service was none other than Captain Wingdale. When I described this gentleman as a retired sea captain, you perhaps got a wrong idea of him. He is not retired due to his age but due to having cornered enough prize money that he no longer requires the salary paid by the Royal Navy. I cannot think more than a handful of men in the whole kingdom actually *enjoy* to spend their lives at sea on a bouncing deck, with a tightly restricted company. Wingdale was in his early forties, still in the prime of life. He was dark haired, ruddy of complexion, with deep lines around his eyes, which I imagine to have been formed from looking into the sun to read the weather. He was broad-shouldered, of military bearing, but with, of course, no uniform. The "Captain" is an honourary title now. He wears jackets of excellent material and an exaggerated cut, the shoulders padded, the waist too tightly taken in for comfort I am convinced. I suspect a corset might account for that wasp waist that a lady could envy. One has always the impression when looking at him that he is pulling in his stomach and expanding his chest as hard as he can. Such a big, barrel chest is not natural, except in baboons or gorillas. There is nothing amiss in his cunning. He is as shrewd as can stare, and not totally without social graces either, though he is betrayed at times into ungenteel utterances that hint at a past less refined than the present. Oh, and there is no Mrs. Wingdale, which makes him more than tolerable to all families with an aging daughter to be disposed of.

Nora and I were accosted by Tom Carrick. We strolled to within eavesdropping distance of the Nabob and the Captain. Also within nodding distance of the Tartar and Emily, though their heads were kept carefully averted. No nods were exchanged.

"I suppose you will be attending the tea party for Rush-Bearing come next Saturday," Tom said, in his hearty, loud voice.

"Is it that time already?" I asked. Rush-Bearing occurs early in August. It is a festivity that is fast dying out, but at Grasmere it is still done. In the olden days it had a practical purpose — strewing fresh rushes on the church floor — and was done by adults. It has dwindled (since the church now has a stone floor) to a symbolic affair, with children carrying rushes and flowers in a procession to the church, where the minister reads a service. The children sing and are later entertained with a tea-party, also attended by the more ardent adult parishioners. Being a spinster of the parish I am one of the ladies usually stuck to manage the whole affair. It is the singing practice that consumes most of the time. When a spinster has the identical chores of a wife, as I have in managing Ambledown (with a few of the husband's chores thrown in for good measure), I don't know why it is I am thought to have all manner of time free, but so it is. Charities, social gatherings, all these trivial church matters fall upon a handful of us spinsters and widows. I wouldn't be a bit surprised if Eleanor Glover married her husband to escape her share of these dull jobs. I cannot see any other advantage that accrued to her in the match.

"Why, it was announced this morning, Chloe," Tom reminded me. I must have been wool-gathering at the time. I had not heard the announcement.

"Yes, I'll be there," I said, inclining my head to try to hear what was causing Wingdale and Gamble to guffaw as though they were at a men-only rout, when they were still on church property. Everyone was staring at them.

When Nora began speaking to Tom about Edward's trip, I listened quite shamelessly to the other party. Wingdale was inviting Gamble to one of his assemblies. The reply, imperfectly heard, was that Emily might enjoy it.

There was no difficulty in overhearing Emily's opinion. She squealed in delight, in a most unladylike manner that caused the Tartar to silence her with a sharp, "Emily!" The Captain then mentioned some other features of Wingdale Hause, including the meals, which he described as being "something quite out of the ordinary", as indeed they are from all reports. I have never personally deigned to set a toe inside the establishment, and never will. Where else can you pay a guinea for tough roast beef, reheated potatoes, and wine that bears a strong resemblance to turpentine?

There was more loud talking and louder laughing, the whole carried out in voices raised high enough to indicate the speakers' disregard for the opinion of bystanders. This particular brand of arrogance is often practiced by under-bred tourists, but outside of Wingdale himself it has been kept under control amongst the local people. At some point during the conversation, Tom turned around to direct a scowl on the speakers and ended up nodding to Emily, as the gentlemen paid him no heed. This dangerous encroachment of our presence had the effect of the guardians getting rid of Wingdale so they could hustle their ward off home. It was perfectly clear this was their intention— to avoid speaking to us. In a fit of pique I said, in no low voice, that they should put the girl under lock and key to keep her safe till they convinced her to marry her cousin. The cabbage-green eyes narrowed at me, glinting maliciously. I stared back at her but did not intend to be the first to speak. While still staring, I observed from the corner of my eye that Gamble too had overheard my speech. His black head turned slowly, as though he could not quite make up his mind whether to admit it. He exchanged one quick, guilty glance with the Tartar, then turned his obsidian eyes on me.

If looks could kill I would have been destroyed on the spot. He was *furious*, and trying hard to hide it. It didn't take much cunning to realize why. He was angry that I had figured out his strategy with regard to Emily, his plan to subdue her unwillingness with trifling luxuries and social diversions till he could persuade her to have him. "Miss Barwick, is it not?" he asked, after a long moment of subjecting me to his scrutiny.

I nodded and replied in an affable tone, "Mr. Gamble, if memory serves." Next I turned to Emily, deciding to further discommode the guardians with a little teasing. "Emily, how grand you look today. We were all wondering who the Incomparable was in church. We hardly recognized you. You *do* recognize me, I hope? Chloe—Edward's sister. You remember Edward."

She blushed to the roots of her blond curls and muttered, "Good morning, Chloe," then directed a plea for instructions on Mrs. Crawford, who reached out her black mittens to get a physical grasp on the girl's arm, as though I might seize her and carry her off by main force. I could not repress an ironic smile at this, and didn't try very hard either.

"I believe your chaperones are anxious for your safe-keeping, Emily. I shan't detain you longer. Good morning." I swept a general curtsey in the direction of their party, took Tom's arm for support to my nervous legs, and left, while my escort inveighed against the bad manners being practiced by "certain people who should know better." In my state I thought he meant myself, but further remarks showed it to be Gamble's group he had in mind.

I did not expect to see those certain bad-mannered people

again till next Sunday, unless it happened they were met in the village. To my considerable surprise, two of them descended on us that same afternoon at Ambledown, about two hours after luncheon. We sat in the garden under a spreading copper beech tree, gasping in the heat of a warmer than usual summer. Poor Edward would be sweltering as he clambered over the fells. When I saw a little blue phaeton darting down the road, pulled by a pair of cream ponies, I took the notion a travelling group of players had come to town. Nothing else in my experience could account for so lively a turn-out. It was not long dawning on me (as soon, in fact, as a blonde lady and a dark gentleman were descried) that the couple were from Carnforth Hall. "On their way in to Wingdale Hause for a piece of stringy mutton," I said to Nora.

"Too early. It is some social call. Perhaps he is taking Emily to visit Lady Irene Castleman. Tom mentioned at church that she is back."

I appeared to have missed quite a bit of gossip at church, but I disliked to admit it. It was not unusual for Lady Irene to visit her summer home on the lake, however. She usually came for a few months every year to escape the tedium of a summer in London. She was some kin by marriage to Lord Carnforth, married a cousin of his, I believe. She was a widow, one of those aging ladies determined to be youthful till she snares another husband. I fancy it was a hard job to keep up any semblance of youth, but she had nothing more demanding to do with her time. No tea parties at the church for her.

I don't know which of us was the more surprised when the carriage slowed down to make the turn off to Ambledown. We are situated at the crest of a gentle slope, which gives us a good view of the road below. "They're coming here!" Nora exclaimed in horror.

"So they are. Perhaps we are to be arrested for living so close to them, and possessing a bachelor relation."

"What the deuce can they want?" This was low talk of a sort not generally indulged in by Mrs. Whitmore, to say 'deuce.'

"We'll soon know," I advised, as the sound of wheels and

47

hooves was heard approaching at a good clip. We said no more while we waited the sixty seconds or so for the carriage to appear around the bend. "Why, it is *Emily* driving!" I exclaimed in surprise. The reason for my surprise was that Emily had never been known to drive so much as a gig in her entire life, and here was she suddenly holding the reins to a pair of very lively steppers. Her inexperience was not hard to read. She let the team continue its advance till both Nor and myself, to say nothing of the copper beech, were in some danger of being bowled over. Then Gamble made a grab for the reins and wrestled the team to a halt. Nora and I were both in flight for our lives by this time.

The exciting manner of their arrival robbed me of a chance to give them the chilly reception I had been preparing. I had intended asking Mr. Gamble if he was seeking directions to Lady Irene's cottage, but was side-tracked to ask him if he were mad, instead, to come charging at us full tilt. When the animals were got under control, he hopped down and assisted Emily from her perch, in no very decorous way, swinging her around to show a good four inches of lovely lace on her petticoats. The stable boy came running at the racket and was asked to stable the carriage.

Before it was taken away Emily began babbling out her disjointed story. "See the pretty phaeton Cousin John has given me, Chloe, and the team. Aren't they beauties? They are called Jill and Judy. They're my very own."

"How nice. You will be perfectly free to go wherever you wish —or are *allowed*—now, Emily," I complimented her, with never a glance at her imprisoner.

"After she learns to handle the ribbons," Gamble said quickly.

"Cousin John is teaching me. It is so hard!" she said, with a happy sigh, as she went forward to pat her team goodbye. "The secret is not to tug at the reins," she confided, "but when I get frightened, I can't seem to help doing it."

"It is only a knack. You'll soon get used to it," Nora assured her. "If *I* learned to do it, *you* can. What I never did master is riding."

"That is the next item on our agenda," Gamble said,

strolling forward in a casual fashion, like any polite visitor. I thought I detected some less polite quality not far beneath the surface, but perhaps I was imagining. He took up a vacant chair beside me, while I turned to congratulate Emily on the liveliness of her team.

"Like your tinker's wagon," she said, laughing, and acting more like her old self than when the Tartar was along. "It was black when John bought it, but when I told him how prettily you and Edward had done up your landau, he had the servants paint it any shade I wanted. I chose blue. There were little brass bells to go on it, but they frightened the horses so I took them off. They are from India," she added, with a warm smile for Cousin John, who had been, if you recall, 'that horrid Jack Gamble' a few days previously. He was obviously having very good luck with his scheme of buttering her into compliance. Perhaps even into love.

"I understand your cousin has brought many strange objects back from India."

"Oh, Edward told you about Lord Simian!" she exclaimed.

"He never mentioned a word about any lord!" Nora exclaimed at once, full of curiosity. I mentioned, I think, that she was a little keener on aristocracy than I can quite like.

"That is my dear little monkey, you must know," Emily told her. "Such a clever rascal as he is. He eats right out of my hand."

"I would be very careful of germs if I were you, Emily," I told her. "Do the tiger and elephant eat out of your hand too?"

"No, though they will take food from John."

"I am careful of germs, Miss Barwick," he said to my back, for I had not yet turned to address any remark to him.

Nora, easily pacified, asked him what he planned doing with these wild beasts. "No idea," he admitted shamelessly.

"Your new friend, Captain Wingdale, will doubtlessly have some good commercial idea," I advised him. "A zoo out behind Wingdale Hause, perhaps, to amuse those who tire of attending assemblies every night of the week. A pity he put up a coat of arms before he knew about the elephant. That would have been a unique addition to the sign."

"There is no assembly on Sunday, Chloe," Emily told me. 'John is going to take me tomorrow night."

"How very considerate your cousin is."

"Indeed he is! He gives me everything." She turned her eyes towards him, eyes glowing with some emotion which was perhaps not yet love, but certainly admiration bordering on love. She was blooming like a hothouse rose, with a flush on her cheeks to match the glow in her eyes. She reminded me of a gentle bloom being forced open before its time by the excessive heat of Gamble's hothouse wooing. Clearly that was what was going on. There was some febrile quality in her that was unnatural. Excitement, prolonged excitement, I judged to be the cause of it.

It must be surpassingly exciting for her now, I thought. Accustomed to little company and less luxury, she was suddenly inundated with both. I stole a quick glance to see how Gamble was behaving towards her. He sat staring towards Ambledown. Seeing the house through another's eyes, I was struck most miserably with its shabby appearance. It struck me as odd, though, that he paid no attention to Emily. Perhaps I frowned. I know at least that I was still watching him when he glanced up and caught me at it. To cover my little gêne I said, "Very warm weather we are having this summer."

"Warm?" he asked. "I was just enjoying the pleasant coolness. It seems nearly cold to me, after Calcutta."

"This is the warmest summer we've had in a decade."

"Very likely."

Nora initiated some chat with Emily. He listened for only a moment before turning back to me. "Will you show me around the place, Miss Barwick?" he asked.

"There is not much to see. My brother and I raise Herdwick sheep, you know. They are up grazing on the fells."

"I would like an opportunity to talk to you in private," he said impatiently, as though I should have guessed the hidden meaning, with nothing to indicate it.

"Why did you not say so? Would you like to go indoors?"

"No, no, we shall walk about a little," he said quietly, with a look towards Emily. He did not wish her to realize what he was about, in other words.

Swelling with curiosity, I arose at once and walked back towards the orchard with him, after telling Nora that Mr. Gamble was curious to have a look at the estate. "What is it you want to discuss?" I asked.

"Emily and myself," he answered. "I could not help overhearing you in the church yard this morning. The nature of your remarks . . ."

"I am surprised you could hear anything over Captain Wingdale's bellowing. Such a raucous, uncouth voice as he has," I added gently, but I think he knew he had spoken as loudly.

"I have good ears. Perhaps you would be kind enough to tell me whether what you said is being generally repeated, by anyone but yourself."

"You mistake the matter if you think I have nothing better to do than gossip about my neighbours. I have said nothing about either you or Emily, except for the one remark I made within your hearing. If others have said so, they have not said it to me."

"An inappropriate spot you chose for your one outbreak. Do I have your assurance you will not repeat that remark?"

"I do not owe you any assurance on anything, Mr. Gamble. This request is nothing short of an insult. If Emily has decided not to have Edward, it is entirely . . ."

"Edward has not asked her to marry him. I hope he does not mean to do so. The match is utterly ineligible, or so I judge from what I have seen and heard."

"I cannot imagine what gossip you have heard that leads you to believe Edward to be beneath a penniless lady of extremely mediocre accomplishments and no talents except for appearing pretty. The Barwicks are an old and well-respected family, sir."

"I do not judge by gossip," he said, cutting me off before I could mention our various prestigious ancestors. "I know from prime sources that Edward has no income save what he makes from Ambledown. I know the extent of his mortgage and can only marvel that you keep up as respectable an appearance as you do. I know as well that he is no manager. There is little like-lihood of his pulling himself up by his bootstraps, as a different sort of go-getting gentleman might do. He is a poet, I understand?''

"Yes, and a good one," I shot back angrily, and inaccurately.

"Does he make much money at it?''

"When a man is a poet, money is of little interest to him."

"That's what I was afraid of. He has no blunt, and no practi-cal ability to make any. Emily is in the same predicament. You must see this is a wretched match for you to be pushing on them."

"*I* pushing on them! Well upon my word, this surpasses all the rest. That girl came here hounding him to death, throwing her cap at him day after day, making handkerchiefs.... And now to say *I* pushed it, when I have advised Edward a dozen times against it!''

"You must confess when first I came here I was given to understand the match had your sanction."

"No, sir, you were given to understand I resented your heavy-handed manner of dealing with the affair."

"Ah good, then I have misunderstood your feelings. I thought I sensed some resentment of my courting Emily."

"It is nothing to me one way or the other. The romance, or whatever it was between Emily and Edward, was of their own devising. You will not find me throwing any rubs in your way, though I must say it is odd Emily should encourage you when she has been chasing Edward as hard as she can any time these past months."

"Boredom," he explained curtly. "She is a romantical girl, her head full of fellows, and no one to carry on with now that he's gone. If it had not been Edward, it would have been some-one even more ineligible. You must realize a match between them is impossible. Send your brother to me when he returns, and we'll talk it over. He cannot be very eager to have her in any case, or he would not have gone racketing off to climb the rocks for a month at this time. If he did not recognize me for competi-tion, he should at least have realized he needed to win my approval of his suit."

As we were both being so frank, I decided to settle firmly how matters stood. "Is it your intention to marry Emily then?"

He stopped walking. We had reached the end of the orchard and were looking off to the fells behind—still beautiful, even in the bracken season, though not so beautiful as at some other times. Dots of moving gray and white could be picked out, the sheep scrabbling about for food. After a longish pause, he said, "Maybe," in the most unemotional tone imaginable. He might have been a farmer discussing those sheep, except that farmers are usually more concerned than he appeared to be. I waited to hear what provisos stood in the way. "I mean to marry some nice proper lady in any case, and do it soon," he added, with his back still towards me.

I said nothing, but I was wondering whether his infatuation with the girl had not begun to fade already. This was not the voice of the man who had teased her in our saloon the day he came to take her home. I don't know why it was, but Lady Irene Castleman flitted into my head. I daresay it was Nora's mention that she was again amongst us, along, of course, with her relentless pursuit of any eligible male, that gave rise to the thought. When he turned back to me, his face was changed, transformed into an expression of reverence. An expression it had not worn in church, I might add, but one often seen on admirers of the fells.

"I mean to settle down at last, you see. I never looked to be Carnforth. There was another cousin..."

"Wilbur Gamble," I said.

"That's the one. Old Wilbur. I made sure he'd live forever, or at least till he had produced a dozen sons. Well, he didn't, so it is up to me. I'll have to be the village worthy, instead of the wild buck I once was. A good, decent wife seems the right first step, don't you think?"

"It would do something to mitigate...that is..."

"My scarlet past is known, is it? Even to non-gossipers," he added with a glinting light of irony in his eyes. "I had better find this good woman without delay."

"I have lived here all my life. It is impossible not to be privy to the more colourful stories of the neighbourhood. I know no details, and don't wish to know any. When a gentleman has picked up a shady reputation, however, he can often dilute it by a good marriage."

"Quite. That is why I wish no gossip, no scandal about my relationship with Cousin Emily. She is not being coerced to have me, if that is what you actually think. Whether we marry or not, I don't wish the girl's reputation damaged, and of course my own is also of concern to me."

"Of equal concern must be the state Carnforth Hall is in," I pointed out.

"That is remediable. A gent don't come home from India poor, if he has his wits about him."

"A pity Edward could not get a position there," I commented, really to myself, as Gamble had turned away again to soak up the beauty of the landscape.

"I said if he has his wits about him, Miss Barwick," he said over his shoulder.

"Edward is not actually feeble-minded. Just young. He will grow out of this phase."

"I hope so, for your sake as well as his own. Indeed for the sake of the neighbourhood. It is a pity to see Ambledown so sadly deteriorated. It is one of the finer old historical homes in the district. Older than the Hall, I think?"

"Yes, I believe the Barwicks were here for some time before the Gambles arrived," I was happy to tell him.

"It really is a shame," he said rather wistfully, then shook the thought away and returned to the present situation. "What you inferred about Emily being restrained in some manner by us, it is not true. She is free to come and go as she likes, within the bounds of propriety of course. She has led an incredibly sequestered life. I plan to take her about a little into good society— London next spring for the Season, and before that to visit and attend any local parties that offer. She is free to visit you, if she wishes, and we hope you will also come to see her at the Hall."

This was not so magnanimous a course as it sounded, for Edward was not here this month. Neither was there much in the way of attractive gentlemen locally to lure her from him. As to

London, that was half a year away or more. If Carnforth were not dead by that time, making the visit impossible due to mourning, I would be surprised.

"Will you come?" he asked impatiently, breaking into my reverie.

"I am very busy. We are not much in the custom of visiting Emily at her home. Usually she came to see us here."

"You actually run Ambledown yourself?"

"Yes. I do not personally shear the sheep and mend the stone walls, but I handle the accounting and generally deal with any problem that arises."

"That must keep you busy," he murmured, turning back towards the house, to Emily and Nora. As we proceeded he mentioned the many changes he noticed since his return—the empty houses where families had moved out, the number of tourists, the seeming busyness of the place, yet without any great prosperity.

"There is plenty of prosperity, most of it in your friend Wingdale's pockets," I answered sharply.

"That's the kind of friends I live to have," he answered, laughing lightly. Unfortunately, he did not turn to see the sneer I was directing at him.

"For Emily as well as yourself?" I was forced to enquire, to get him to look at me.

"Oh yes," he agreed readily. "For Emily even more than myself. I don't expect that custom has changed in the fifteen years I have been away. So far as I have heard, pretty ladies of good breeding and narrow means still marry gentlemen of fortune, if they are wise and lucky."

I cast a withering look on him, but we had rounded the corner of the house, and he was looking to Emily, so he missed it. During our absence Nora had called for lemonade. I expect Mr. Gamble would have preferred a stronger drink. He accepted the lemonade like a gentleman, however, and gulped it down before calling for the blue phaeton.

We waved goodbye as they jogged off, the cream ponies already getting away from Emily's control so that Gamble had to put an arm around her shoulder to get at the reins. He had devised a singularly successful means of courting his cousin. Emily's merry laughter drifted back on the wind.

"They'll be married before Edward gets back," I prophecied.

"She does seem fond of him," Nora admitted. "But I cannot think she *loves* him, Chloe. She spoke of Edward all the time the two of you were gone. What did Gamble want?"

"To whitewash the scandalous way he is trapping Emily into marrying him. I'm going to shell the peas while we sit out here, Nora. I hate being idle."

═ 7 ═

RAIN IS USUALLY a prominent feature of our Lake District. This summer it was remarkably dry and hot. The dust nearly choked me as I rumbled into Grasmere in the tinker's wagon to practice the children's songs for the Rush-Bearing. The town was swarming with tourists, spilling out of Wingdale Hause into the various shops to purchase souvenirs, maps, sweets. A street vendor hawked ices. They came ostensibly to admire the lakes and fells. Why the deuce did they not go and look at them then, and leave the stores and streets for the inhabitants of the place?

They also came in droves to see our church, which is one of the most beautiful and interesting in the district, in my humble opinion. Dating from the eleventh century (and possibly as much as four centuries older), it is dedicated to St. Oswald. The tourists, added to the children come for practice, made access to the church nearly impossible. Miss Johnson and Mrs. Ostler were the other spinster and widow who were to assist me in the Rush-Bearing rehearsal.

It was a tedious enough afternoon to be sure. I did not much look forward to the dusty drive home either. It was Miss Johnson's suggestion that we stop in at the Windgale Hause tea shop for some refreshment before making the trip. As she lived not two streets away, I wondered that she did not invite us into her own home. "For it is so lively there, you know," she said in a shamefaced way.

To my astonishment Mrs. Ostler expressed no surprise at this notion of paying Captain Wingdale for a cup of tea. "Lovely," she gushed. (It was to be Miss Johnson's treat, you see, to make up for not having us to her own house.)

"I do not frequent Wingdale's place," I said icily.

"Everyone does, Chloe," Miss Johnson informed me. "Even Lady Emily is going nowadays, attending the assemblies with her cousin, you know."

"Every night?" I asked in horror, for I knew of course she was to have gone on the Monday.

"Not every night," Miss Johnson answered. "Twice they have been, on Monday and Thursday."

This talk was held on Friday, the eve of the Rush-Bearing ceremony.

"Her cousin is always with her," Mrs. Ostler rattled on. "They say there will be a match in that quarter. What happened to her and Edward, Chloe?"

"Edward is touring."

"When the cat's away, the mouse will play," Miss Johnson informed me, with great unoriginality and great satisfaction. "Well, do you come with us or not?"

"No, I must get home," I said evasively, for I had really nothing of any urgency to do. I would sit out under the copper beech, mending while Nora netted.

My mood was not of the best as I clipped along the road home. Neither did it improve when I met the little blue phaeton nipping into town, with Emily handling the ribbons somewhat more capably than before. Plenty of practice. Gamble sat by her side. He lifted a hand in salute and would have stopped, I think, had I given any indication of doing so. I did not, but bowled past as fast as Belle would carry me, to lick my wounds and wonder that the old natives who had been here forever could turn traitor and give Wingdale their patronage. Next thing we heard, they would be deserting the church dance Saturday night and going to Wingdale's assembly instead of supporting local charities (for the funds from the Rush-Bearing party go to charity).

When Tom came out to Ambledown on that Friday evening, I was in a mood to be kind to him. I accepted his offer to attend the church dance next evening with him, and asked him to dine with Nora and myself before it, as he would be at the afternoon

do, and this would save him the trip home. He read more encouragement into the offer than I had intended. I had to become quite sharp when Nora, the gudgeon, coyly excused herself to "just run upstairs a minute" that lasted half an hour,
long enough for him to move over to join me on the sofa. As I
slid by degrees the twelve inches towards its far end, he slid right
along after me, and soon had his arms around me.

I like Tom, as I have indicated. What I could not like was to
be in his arms. To feel his soft lips groping for mine was a thing
so downright repellent I regretted having accepted the offer to
the dance. Yet there was not a thing wrong with him. He was
clean shaven, his personal habits unexceptionable. What re-
pelled was the mere physical closeness of him. "You're an *unnatural* girl, Chloe," he said, offended.

"I have a headache, Tom," I excused. Lord, how could
women go marrying men and give them *carte blanche* to do this
any time they wished? I would as soon be kissed by a Herdwick.

He flew into a fit of pique and soon took his leave, asking in a
voice heavy with sarcasm if I was quite sure my headache would
be cured by Saturday night. How I wished to tell him it would
not! I wanted to take back my promise, to be completely and
utterly free of him, but I looked at his kind, offended face and
said nothing of the sort. "Quite sure, but if you have changed
your mind about taking me, Tom . . ."

"You know I didn't mean that!" A kiss on the hand was en-
durable. He left, mollified, even apologizing for that timid
attempt at love-making. Was *that* what I found so off putting?
Was he *too* biddable? I tried to envisage Tom being more force-
ful, insistent, holding me in his arms by force. No image would
come. Instead what popped into my head was Jack Gamble. *He*
was not a man to be put off by any weak claim of a headache. I
felt it instinctively. I felt too it would be difficult, impossible,
for Emily to stave him off if he decided to have her. It seemed
downright *wrong*, what he was doing, yet when a man's intentions are marriage, the world does not call it wrong, but honour-
able. Maybe they could be happy together after all.

Other than passing them on the road that afternoon, I had

not seen them together since last Sunday's visit. I had not gone to the Hall, and they had not returned to Ambledown, but local gossip said they were constantly together. Outside of Edward's concern in the matter, I decided I did not much care. I walked into the hallway and shouted up the stairs, "You can come down now, Auntie. He's gone."

"Already?" she called over the bannister. "He didn't stay long."

"He had a headache," I told her, to prevent being sent to bed with a powder, as I would have been had I claimed the headache for my own.

The Rush-Bearing was a great success. Not only the locals attended in full number, but the tourists as well came to have a look at this quaint custom. Lady Irene Castleman was in town for the occasion. She came to the tea party afterwards, looking very much out of place amongst the less fashionable ladies present. She had once been an extremely pretty woman, just a hair's breadth short of beautiful. She is still attractive, with her coppery hair, her painted cheeks and her wide smile. My own preference, had I been a male of mature years, would be an interesting lady like Irene, as opposed to a young, silly chit like Emily. But then my age perhaps inclines me to choose mind over body. She wore an elegant gown of sea green to match her eyes and contrast superbly with her hair.

"Still at it, eh, Chloe?" she asked, in her throaty voice.

"As you see, Lady Irene. Cream and sugar?" I poured at one of the tea tables.

"Clear, please. I am watching my figure. No one else will if I don't. I hear Jack Gamble is back at the Hall."

"Yes, he returned a few weeks ago."

"Interesting," she said, with a saucy smile, not even attempting to disguise her interest. "How is old Carnforth?"

"Ailing, as usual."

"I must pay my respects. Where is Edward? I have not seen him since I arrived. I heard some talk of his seeing my cousin, Emily."

I explained Edward's tour, but she knew it already. She was interested in Jack Gamble and wanted to hear from the horse's sister's mouth how affairs stood with Emily and Edward. What her chances were with Gamble, in other words. In mid-sentence, she spotted him and interrupted me.

"Ah, there is dear little Emily now. What a sweet child it is!"

She was off like a hound after a fox. Looking after her, I noticed the sweet child was accompanied by her male cousin. It was the cousin (male) who was soon having his hand seized by Lady Irene. As the pressure of business allowed, I kept an eye on the three of them for the next while. I swear Lady Irene's mouth never stopped flying. When Gamble and Emily came for their tea, she was still with them, gabbling away, urging Emily (who would hardly go alone) to come and visit her. I examined Jack closely to see how he was enjoying her company. He wore an amused, interested look. I felt if only Lady Irene would close her mouth occasionally she might have better luck.

"Nice show, Miss Barwick," Jack Gamble said, when he reached his brown hand out for his tea cup. "It is good to see the old traditions being kept up. Will there be a dance this evening, as there used to be in the old days?"

"Yes, the locals will attend, Mr. Gamble, though you perhaps would be more interested in Captain Wingdale's assembly."

"You forget I am a local, ma'am. Cream, no sugar, please," he said, still holding out his cup. The cream was as close to his hand as my own, but I have often remarked that a gentleman likes to have a good deal of service. Edward will sit till the pot grows cold sooner than he will pour his own tea. My father, too, was the same.

"You have not called on us," he said, still waiting for his cream. I gave in, and poured for him. "Thank you," he said, looking over his shoulder to determine he was the last in the line.

"I have been rather busy this week."

"When does that brother of yours return?"

"Not for two weeks."

"A laggard in love," he commented idly, just as Tom strolled up to me. The glance managed to include Tom in the statement just made, though Edward was the prime target.

"Hello, Chloe. How are you feeling? I hope that headache that bothered you last night is gone," Tom said, smiling to indicate all was forgiven.

I cannot imagine why I should have been made to feel foolish at his speech, unless it was due to the ironic smile Jack Gamble chose to bestow on me. It was the strangest thing, almost as though he *knew* why I had assumed the migraine.

"All gone. You have not forgotten you are coming to us for dinner, Tom?" I asked, smiling as brightly as I could.

"Certainly not. I had my man take my evening clothes on over to Ambledown to change for the party. Well, this looks like a pretty good do," he rambled on, glancing about for a chair. There was one against the wall behind me. He went to get it, leaving Gamble still at the tea table with me.

"Headache, eh?" he said, cocking his head at a bold angle and laughing. "Tch, tch, and you are not even married yet," he added, then strolled off to rejoin Lady Irene and Emily, as Tom dragged the chair to my side. Wingdale had entered while my interest was diverted elsewhere. He did not come for tea, but went to stand at Lady Irene's side, his tongue all but hanging out in admiration.

"Seems as though Lady Irene has found her match at last," Tom said.

He was not so finely attuned to affairs of the heart as a lady is. It was clear to the most uninterested observer that while Wingdale was falling over himself to be civil to Lady Irene, the lady had smiles for no one but Jack. Before long she had detached him from the others to go and admire the newly-laid rushes. Emily came up to me to ask if I had heard from Edward. I told her I had not.

"I had a note," she confessed, with a delightful blush that affected even Tom, no indiscriminate admirer of ladies as a rule. Had I cared for him at all, I might have felt a pang of jealousy.

"A poem it was," she went on. "I'll bring it over for you to read tomorrow, if you are free, Chloe."

"Yes, I am free."

She left, with a wave of her fingers, to rush after Jack and Irene. "A bit of a shame for that poor little creature to be living with Jack Gamble," Tom said. "She'll end up hitched to him, when it is plain as a pikestaff it is Edward she loves."

As I watched her putting a possessive hand on Jack's arm, smiling at him ever so sweetly, I found her hard to pity. She was an innocent minx, and while she seemed to have some feelings for Edward, it was rather clear she was also jealous of Lady Irene.

8

YOU MAY HAVE got the idea that Jack Gamble was no slouch in his dealings with the opposite sex. He was a sloth when set beside his cousin, Lady Irene. Tom had come to the Rush-Bearing with his evening clothes packed. It turned out Lady Irene had pulled the same stunt, but without the excuse of any invitation to stay anywhere. I later learned from Emily that Irene had packed a case as well, intending, if all else failed, to stay a few nights at Wingdale Hause, but her real goal was Carnforth Hall. She achieved it. By some means unknown to Emily (and hence to myself) she angled an invitation from Gamble to remain a few days with them.

She entered the dancing party on his arm, looking like an orchid on the verge of decay, but still pretty. The reason I say orchid is that she wore a chiffon creation, all filmy, with lace of that violet shade commonly associated with orchids. It took some nerve to select that particular hue with her copper curls, but it worked. Emily, on Gamble's other side, was quite cast into the shade, a blushing primrose. It was soon clear that the older lady was falling heir to the better part of Gamble's attention.

It was she who stood up with him for the opening minuet, while Emily was handed over to Ian Welter, the editor of a quarterly poetry magazine who summers in our midst. He has not the taint of the tourist, as his family has had a cottage here forever. Nor did Irene let her quarry go at the minuet's end. She had confirmed her fears of a match between the two cousins, and was at pains to keep them apart. It was her plan, I believe, to show herself as a much admired, popular Lady Bountiful in the district. She was so gracious and condescending to us all I felt like pulling her red curls out.

"Hello, Chloe," she said, wafting by with Gamble securely tethered at her side. "Such a charming party. You are to be congratulated."

"Thank you, but I do not take credit for the whole, Lady Irene."

"Tom," she went on, turning to him while I was still objecting to her congratulations. "How is your dear mama? I must drop over and see her soon. Give her my regards."

Before he could say he would, she had pulled Gamble on to the next group. I could not hear her comments, but I could see her smile, see her squeezing of fingers, her little dying look to Gamble—as though to say, "Forgive me, but I must recognize my people. It is expected of me." A pity he had not glanced behind her to see the astonished faces watching her performance. He did not do so, however. His looks were all for Irene. He wore the satisfied air of a man who knows he has the prettiest lady in the room at his side. He did not once look to see how Emily fared.

Nora was nodding wisely. The match would have her approval, as it left Lady Emily free to bestow her distinction on Ambledown. I had thought it would have my approval too, but I found myself unhappy with it. She was manipulating him, that was part of it. Of equal disappointment to me was that he was so easily gammoned. I would have thought a man of the world would be more discerning.

He did not get back to Emily till the country dances struck up. Irene was a little long in the tooth to relish these boisterous frolics, so she graciously remembered Emily then, and sat smiling nobly on the pair. I believe business was poor at Wingdale Hause that night. At about eleven Wingdale himself joined our entertainment. To be more specific, he joined Lady Irene, who did not repress his fawning advances as she should have. He danced attendance on her in a servile, cringing, encroaching way. It is my firm belief the pair of them were laughing at the rest of us, looking and pointing and laughing at our country get-ups and country manners. If she thought to incite Gamble to jealousy with this suitor, she was out. He did not like it one bit, but it was anger rather than jealousy that was the cause of his displeasure.

I needed no encouragement to despise Captain Wingdale. When he happened to look in my direction, then nod a salutation, I turned my head away quickly.

"Bloody upstart," said faithful Tom.

When the country dances were over, Irene arose and began drifting towards her cousins once again. "She means to palm that sailor off on Emily and snare Gamble again," Nora said. She was an integral part of our party, sharing all our disgust and animadversions.

"She shan't then," Tom said manfully, and nipped smartly in ahead of them to claim Emily for his partner for the next set.

I made sure Irene would throw custom to the winds and ensnare Gamble for another dance. He was bent on propriety, however, and cast about the hall for a familiar face. Finding none but my own, he settled for me. It was a waltz, thus allowing more conversation than the formal sets.

"I had not realized Lady Irene was remaining for the dance," I said leadingly, to gauge his reaction.

"Yes, she is staying with us for a few days. She wishes to see something of old Carnforth, as this will likely be his last summer."

I enquired for the old gentleman's health and he answered, "He is still hanging on, making it demmed difficult to get anything done."

"What do you mean?"

"I want to get on with repairing the house, but he objects to everything. I had arranged for an architect to come down and repair the statue gallery, but he forbids it."

"It is *his* estate," I pointed out.

"For the time being. It will soon be mine, and in the interim I don't much relish living in pretentious squalor, as you so accurately described it on our first visit. There is plenty to be done outside, and I am going ahead with that. He never sets his nose outside the door."

Nothing else of the least interest passed between us during the waltz. Gamble was light-footed, a good dancer. He told me the English Raj had frequent dancing parties in India. Just before returning to Tom to claim Emily, he repeated the invitation to the Hall. We left the party a little early, as Tom had several miles to drive before he reached home.

I was curious to learn how affairs were progressing at the Hall with Emily and Irene competing for Jack's time, but I had no real notion of paying a visit. On Monday, Emily ventured out alone (but for a groom) in her phaeton and came to call on us. Nearly our first question had to do with Irene.

"She is helping Cousin John choose new decorations for the saloon," she told us. "He is eager to get cleaning it up, and they are choosing new drapery material and upholstery for the sofas today. Irene thinks green is nice."

"It will suit the color of her hair," I said in an innocent voice.

"Yes," Emily replied artlessly. It seemed she was in love with Edward today. She spoke of him for some minutes, then said, "John is taking us to the assembly in Grasmere tonight. Irene wants to go. She mentioned you might like to come with us, Chloe."

I would not have been more surprised had Irene suggested I move into the Hall, like herself. My former dealings with her had been of the slightest. I firmly declined the offer, but continued puzzling over it long after Emily had left. The woman was so devious it took me an hour to figure out her strategy. She wished to encourage the speculation that Emily was heavily embroiled with Edward, you see. Edward's sister being towed along would suggest it to the townfolk, which left Gamble free for herself.

Undaunted by my refusal, she came calling with Emily on Tuesday (giving no mention of ever returning to her own home, I might add). The chatter was all of Edward and poetry. She did so admire Mr. Wordsworth. She never could look at a daffodil without thinking of his delightful poem. She would pay a visit to Dove Cottage one of these days, to see where Wordsworth used to live, in Grasmere. There was nothing so romantic as a poet, was there? She smiled fondly on Emily. Then she harkened back to her first marriage, to introduce the subject of

young love. She was positively shameless, and perfectly successful. Before they left, Emily asked in a wan, yearning little voice
if we thought Edward might return earlier than four weeks. He
had said, in his note to her, that the trip was not so enjoyable as
he had anticipated.

She knew more of how he was faring than we did ourselves.
But I had no real concern for him. The fells are deceptive, even
treacherous. They appear innocent to the tourist, who may set
out in the flush of dawn telling his companions he will be back
for lunch, only to disappear till evening, often having to be
searched for. Edward was born and bred here. He knew their
danger, would take no chances. He would have his compass and
maps. So long as he was back at the end of August to sign the
cheque for the mortgage, I had no fear. That there would be
sufficient funds in the bank to cover the cheque was always a
matter of concern, but one that had little to do with Edward.

Our fleeces had brought a good enough price, but the hot,
dry season was taking its toll of our ready cash. Those plaguey
tourists distressed the sheep farmers by feeding every mooching
sheep who stared at them as they passed, thus encouraging them
to loiter about the roadway waiting for a hand-out—and as
often as not being injured by a carriage. The foxes, our old ene-
mies, were rife, claiming more than their usual share of the
herd, often choosing the ewes who were carrying a lamb and
thus depriving us of two heads at one killing.

These were but incidental, occasional losses. The real de-
stroyer was the wide variety of diseases. The blow-fly, for instance,
which thrives in the bracken, can lay masses of maggots that kill
a sheep in two days by eating its flesh. There are also tape-
worms, ticks, liver-fluke. If the soil is not of the proper sort,
they become souted, losing weight, sickening, and eventually
dying. The silly creatures also become crag-bound, eat vegeta-
tion they should not and bloat up, dying if they are not pierced
to let out the gas. There—I hope you are not sick to your stomach with this recital, but it gives you some idea of the precarious
nature of our livelihood, and the expense of raising sheep.

The cure for some of these ailments is dipping. The blow-fly were particularly severe this hot season, so that there was an extra dipping required. This involved gathering up all our herd from the fells and pike, bringing them down to the sheep-dip for an individual dousing—a procedure abhorrent to the sheep. Many men have to be hired for these boon days, costing a great deal of money.

At Ambledown we were subject to another unforeseen expenditure. Our stone walls, built eons ago and an interesting feature of the fells, took to crumbling on us. At three-and-sixpence for ten yards (the day's work of one man) the job promised to be ruinous. Ruin comes so easily when you are perched on the very edge of solvency. There is some damage to the walls every year due to frost, but ours suffered so much and so late in the season, well past spring, that I began to wonder whether a human hand were not tearing the stones loose, letting our herd wander into precarious perches and, worse, into precarious clover, which can cause death if it is not looked after. We had lost several by this means.

At the back of my mind there lurked the suspicion, perfectly unfounded, that Wingdale was the evil agent, devising a new tactic to get Ambledown away from us. He could hardly go on burning down barns forever, when folks were beginning to voice their suspicions. In any case, I placed implicit trust in our chief shepherd, Geoff Ulrich, who had been with my father for ten years before I was born. Certainly Wingdale had not got to him, whatever he had done about anyone else.

It was Ulrich who first suggested to me that the stone walls were being tampered with. He had seen no one tinkering with them, but from long years on the fells he knew the signs of the marauding work of raw nature and suspected that some other source was responsible for our damage. I am an inveterate roamer of the fells. It is one of life's chief delights for me to set out in the early morning (for later it will be too warm) and walk for an hour before breakfast, admiring the lichen, which comes in all shades, the heather, even the bracken—so pale and delicate in May, darkening to emerald as August approaches, and finally turning from gold to bronze. One can almost forgive it for poisoning our sheep, for without it the fells would be half nude. As one descends from the heights, the bird-cherry and whitebeam await you in the dales, but only for a brief spring season. Even holly and rowan are encountered occasionally. It was not beauty but necessity that propelled my next visit up the slopes. I had had word from Ulrich of another wall crumbling and must go to have a look at it.

=== 9 ===

I SET OUT for the heaf early, before eight, when the air was still fresh and cool. Heaf, incidentally, is the local name for the piece of fellside claimed by a farm for grazing. The sheep had already come down from the tops of the mountains where they sleep, and had begun grazing their way back up. By evening they would be back atop to sleep. Ulrich was particularly busy that morning, chasing off after a ewe and her lamb. I noticed something amiss, but for a full minute, what was lacking did not strike me. Then I noticed what it was. Why was Ulrich going after the ewe himself? Where was Scout, our Border collie? He usually came bounding up to meet me if he were not employed in any more vital business, his pink tongue curling a welcome. I looked around for a sight of his tawny back, his gleaming coat. Scout had a stunt of crawling on his belly like a fox, when he was going after a runaway, to sneak up on it. I looked all around in a loop of three hundred and sixty degrees, discovering that he was nowhere about.

By this time Ulrich had observed me and came loping down the fellside in that peculiar gait of the hillmen that propels them at top speed without pitching them forward on their noses. The toes are pointed out, the knees bent a little, the body forward. "I've come to have a look at the walls, Ulrich," I told him.

"Catastrophe, Miss," he said simply. Ulrich did not deal in euphemism.

"How bad is it?" I asked in alarm, though I could see from where I stood that it was bad enough to be expensive. I mentally toted up the yards, and pounds.

"Nay, I'm not talking walls, but the collie."

"Where is Scout? I hope he is not sick."

"Yonder," he said, pointing off in the direction from which he had come. His voice would have told me the news, if the flocking buzzards had not. They did not hover so over a living body. I took a step towards the spot.

"Nay, you don't want to see it, Miss. It ain't a pleasant sight."

"What happened?"

"Twas no accident."

"Foxes? Foumarts?" I asked, for if hungry enough these creatures have been known to attack even a dog.

"A bullet," he answered. "I saw him before they got at it," he told me simply, with a wave towards the buzzards. "I'd have buried him, but I had no shovel, and the herd were wandering by then. You'll have a shovel sent up," he said.

"It must have been an accident," was my first reaction. No one would be so low as to shoot a shepherd's dog on purpose. The fox hunting done in this district could account for it. It is not done primarily for sport. It is done on foot, and with guns. Someone had been hunting reynard and had accidentally hit Scout.

"No one hunts foxes in the dead o' night," he pointed out. "Scout was hale and hearty when I tucked in last night. This morning, I found him where you see the birds gathering, yonder. Lured far enough down the slope that I'd not hear the shot."

"I wonder you didn't hear it, Ulrich," I said, though I did not mean to condemn the man. I knew him to be faithful.

"I'm a light sleeper usually," he told me. I discerned some trace of sheepishness about him, strong enough almost to amount to guilt.

"Did you sleep more soundly last night?" I urged.

"I'll confess I did, Miss, for it's bothering my conscience," he blurted out, like a little boy owning up to pilfering the sweet jar. "Last night I had summat to drink."

"Ulrich, that is not like you!" I charged. He likes his ale as well as anyone, but to overindulge while on the job is not at all characteristic of him.

"Nay, Miss. It happened thus. Mr. Gamble, he came walking up the hill to talk to me." I stiffened to complete attention, but remained silent. I could think of no innocent reason why Gamble should seek so unlikely a companion. "About the herd, you see," he added, with a sorry eye.

The Lake District has primarily two occupations, sheep raising, and mining. Carnforth's interest was the latter. There was no logical reason for Gamble to have been talking to Ulrich about sheep. "He says the great gaffer's mines are running out, and he's looking to get into sheep farming. We talked for an hour and more. He knows summat about the subject," Ulrich allowed critically. No one outside of himself is allowed to know more than "summat." My own scarce knowledge would be described by him as "less than summat."

"When did the drinking occur?" I asked, somewhat angrily.

"All along," he admitted freely. "He brought a couple of bottles o' wine with him, and we passed them back and forth, like. I told him about sheeping, and he told me tales of India. Strange tales," he added, shaking his head, as though to determine whether his night had been a dream, or a nightmare.

"Where was Scout while all this was going forth?"

"Rounding up the strays first, then as darkness fell, he curled up in his usual spot. I'd have heard him leave if I'd been clean sober," he admitted manfully.

"Just exactly how drunk did you allow yourself to become?"

"Not downright disguised, as ye might say, Miss. A trifle foxed maybe," he allowed, with a judicious frown to see if he had chosen his word with precision.

"I have a good notion to give him a piece of my mind."

"Twould be better to make your first business finding a replacement for Scout," he suggested. A glance around at the wandering herd showed me the justice of his remark.

A true star sheepdog is worth his weight in gold, and nearly impossible to find when you need one urgently. There had been one particularly fine one at the recent Dog Show Trials that Ulrich had praised to the skies. I was fairly sure it was this one he had in mind now. He was a Border collie like Scout, and a general rounder up of sheep. Ulrich had no good opinion of "fixers," as he called those dogs who hypnotize their sheep with an eye. They stopped the sheep well enough, but one had to go and push it to get it moving again. While I stood wondering what astronomical price would be asked for the replacement, there was a clattering of stones and boulders to announce the approach of someone up the other side of the fell.

I was hardly surprised to see the black head and brown face of Jack Gamble. I thought he might return to see how his drinking crony did this morning. I was in a mood to accuse him of having killed Scout himself, though I had no reason to believe him so stupidly cruel, and he had nothing to gain by doing so.

"Ah, Miss Barwick," he said, striding over the rocks with an easy familiarity with the terrain that is impossible to simulate. It made his origins clear, his upbringing in the Lake District. "I hoped I might meet you. I often see you from a balcony at the Hall, cantering over the rocks. A fine day for a walk, is it not?"

"The fineness of the day is destroyed for me, Mr. Gamble," I answered in a damping way, and with an eye cast off to that spot where ravens had joined the buzzard, honking and gabbling over the carcass of Scout.

"Lost a sheep, have you?" he asked. "Ulrich mentioned some trouble with your stone walls."

"It is a much more precious animal we have lost. Our sheep dog has been killed."

"Is that so? Too bad. I noticed a pair of foxes yesterday. They won't often attack a dog. Was it foxes?"

"No, it was a bullet."

"Shot?" he asked, in a surprised tone. "I am sorry to hear it. The hunters ought not to shoot near where the herd are grazing."

"They don't," I answered curtly.

"How did it happen then? When?"

"Last night, while Ulrich was—*indisposed*, after your visit," I said, throwing all the significance I could contrive into the speech. Ulrich hung his head in shame, making me feel a monster.

Gamble regarded me warily for a moment without speaking, deciding, I suppose, what reply to make to this oblique charge. "It is hardly a tragedy," he said, with a twitching of the shoulders that relegated it to a minor mishap. "You will be in a hurry to find a replacement for Scout."

"Just what I've been telling her," Ulrich said, turning his full attention to Gamble. It is a custom of the lower born male natives to relegate mere females to onlookers when there is serious business to be done. The fact of my being in charge of Ambledown was not of sufficient importance to include me now. "Ritson, over to Stickle Tarn, has a fine breed. It's one of them she wants."

"I will be happy to take you over, Miss Barwick, to make up for having caused Ulrich's indisposition," Gamble offered.

"That's not necessary," I said, brushing the offer aside.

"It's a longer trip than she'd like to make alone, and her brother is away," Ulrich went on, still ignoring my presence. "Tell Ritson it's Becky we want. She showed well at the fair. She'll cost something, but there's no stinting on your dog. If she's wise she'll take the bitch, Becky, so as to breed up her own dogs. I could train them to gather for her. It's poor economy not having a young 'un learning. If we had one now..." he said, his voice petering out while his hands silently finished the statement for him. He flung them out, showing the callouses that had deformed his right hand from the constant pressure of the crook. It hung now over his wrist like an umbrella.

"I don't intend going all the way to Stickle Tarn to buy a dog, Ulrich," I said firmly.

"It's the cost you're worried about," he said, reading my mind, or perhaps the worried lines on my forehead. "Ritson will give you credit." This offending speech at least he directed to myself.

"It's not the cost; it is the time. I'll go to Axels, in the village."

"Nay, I don't want to be stuck with a fixer," he said, in a voice that did not invite argument.

To terminate this unpleasant subject, I said, "It is the wall I have really come to see. I'll arrange a substitute for Scout. Now, show me where the walls are breached, if you please."

Three discrete spots were pointed out, great holes knocked out, plenty wide and low enough to allow sheep to scramble through. Ulrich repeated his thought that the mischief had been done by human hand—at night—as he would have seen anyone about the fells by daylight.

When I turned to go home Gamble walked along beside me, hampering my progress greatly, as I could not like to dart sheep-like down the steep slopes with him beside me. I had to lift my skirts and pick my way daintily, taking longer to get home than I could spare with such a busy day ahead of me, getting some sort of a dog to replace Scout and visiting fence menders to haggle them into a bargain.

I was not very good company for Gamble. He first tried to talk, but with my mind so preoccupied I made only desultory answers, so that he soon gave up trying altogether. He offered his hand solicitously to traverse bumps I would have taken at a leap without his help. This wearying mode of getting home was more tiring than my customary scramble. By slow degrees I abandoned it entirely, without quite noticing what I was about. As I leaped down the last two-foot rock and bounded to the meadow below, I was several yards ahead of Gamble. He came puffing up behind me.

"I must be getting soft," he said. "It is kind of you to slow your pace down, but it would have been kinder to refrain from increasing it as we approached the end of the trail. I used to be pretty good at this, once upon a time."

"You won't be winning any fell races this year."

"I did once, right here at Grasmere. You were too young to remember."

My knowing glance undeceived him as to my memory, or at least knowledge, of that season. "I was pretty unpopular with the local bucks, an outsider pushing in and winning the prize, but over in the west where I come from, the countryside is much wilder than these gentle slopes you have here."

"You were wise to move then, as you can hardly manage these little inclines in your senility. Where exactly was your home?"

He took the rebuke in stiff silence, putting all his displeasure into one scathing look. "The Cumberland coast, where we have the more beautiful, wild scenery," he answered, with that pride that is so much a part of those westerners.

"Most tourists prefer *our* landscape," I retaliated.

"True, but I am surprised to hear Miss Barwick sunk to quoting tourists as a judge. Now that you are speaking to me again, pray permit me to apologize for having got Ulrich tipsy last night. I went to milk him for his knowledge, and felt I should provide something in return. Loll shrub was obviously a poor thing to have provided. I shan't do it again."

"Loll shrub? What on earth is that?"

"It is what we call red wine in India. I am planning to get into sheep farming and know Ulrich to be an expert."

"I would have thought you would turn your time and attention to the copper mine."

"So I would have done, were it not on the verge of running out. Old Carnforth insists it is good for another ten years, but the man I have had in to do surveys for me says otherwise. What bit of ore that remains is too deep and too thin a strain to be mined economically. Besides, I would rather be a farmer. My father raised sheep, so I am not totally ignorant."

"What happened to your father's estate?"

"I sold it after I came back from India—paid off the mortgage and had nearly enough left to buy myself a new jacket in London. The work of Weston. Like it?" he asked, fingering his coat.

"Exquisite." We had reached the house. As I was feeling warm myself, I took for granted Mr. Gamble was also and invited him in for refreshment, to repay his civility in seeing me home. I also wished to find time to work the subject around to Lady Irene, in some subtle manner. He had not mentioned her.

"That sounds delightful. Would it be possible for us to sit in the garden? Yours is so lovely," he said, looking to the left, where a tangle of honeysuckle fought their way to the sun, hampered by sweet peas. There were some dispirited roses in there somewhere.

I physically blushed for the condition of it. "It's a mess," I admitted quite frankly. "I was used to take some pride in it, but lately. ... We are very busy, you know."

He continued looking at it, seeming to inhale its jumbled profusion. "I don't care for these new-fangled gardens where every bloom is placed artistically, all of a new improved variety, and nothing ever to be touched on pain of having your fingers cut off. May I?" he asked playfully, touching a honeysuckle, which he snapped off and smelled before sticking it into his vest.

"Of course. Nothing is improved here."

"My mother had such a garden as this," he said.

I had never thought of Mr. Gamble as having had a mother, which is rather absurd when I put it down in black and white, but you know what I mean. There was nothing of the boy in him—he was all mature man. "There were pretty little purple flowers in the autumn. What would they have been?"

"Asters, perhaps." As he sank into a reverie of his mother's garden, I walked to the backhouse door and called for ale, and a glass of lemonade for myself. We pride ourselves a little on growing lemons. We have the only trees for ten miles around, though of course Wingdale imports the fruit by the barrel. When I returned, I noticed Gamble's gaze had roved from the garden to the house—there was an angled view of the front and the side from where we were sitting. The wistful air was still with him, but I think it was for the fading grandeur of Ambledown now, not his mother's garden. He was too polite to say it, but he was surely thinking what I so often thought myself, that it was a pity to let such a fine home sink into disrepair. It was little better than a derelict in its outward appearance, though I will add it was better preserved within, where women were in charge of its upkeep.

The drinks arrived, carried on a tin tray by Effie, our kitchen servant, who curtsied prettily. Effie always made a good appearance, having been jawed into clean aprons and tidy hair by Nora and me. Never immune to a pretty face, Gamble smiled and made a few jokes with her. It, or something, put him in a good mood. He leaned back with a sigh of luxury and took a deep quaff.

"Miss Barwick," he said suddenly, leaning forward in a businesslike way gentlemen seldom adopt with a lady, "I have a suggestion which your pride is not going to like. I suspect your reluctance to go over to Stickle Tarn and buy Becky has to do with a lack of ready blunt. It was foolish, inconsiderate I mean, of Edward to have gone on his tour without leaving you any emergency funds. I hope you will let me loan you the sum required till he returns. The mishap is my fault, and we are neighbours after all, not strangers."

"No, no, it is not at all necessary," I said quickly. "You are quite mistaken."

"No, Miss Barwick, I ain't," he answered baldly. "No good sheep farmer, which I give you credit for being, would think for two minutes of buying a fixer unless he already had a good general sheep dog. If you plan to have only the one, it is one of Ritson's Border collies you want. I see no other reason for not getting this Becky your shepherd spoke of than lack of blunt. I'll go over to Stickle Tarn and pick her up for you. You won't have the burden of making the trip with me, which is the only other reason for your refusal that *I* can think of."

"It is kind of you to offer. Actually Edward left me plenty of money," I lied glibly, "and if he had not, I have good friends from whom I would be more apt to borrow than from a . . . a . . ." I came to a dead halt. I could suddenly think of no word in the world to finish the statement that would not be an insult to my guest. Instead of helping me out of my dilemma he sat looking, first with interest, then gradually with amusement.

"Yes?" he asked, leaning back to wait.

"A westerner," I finished, with an embarrassed smile.

"I expect that is as bad an insult in your view as what you originally intended saying, but I can hardly take exception to the term."

"You must learn to despise anyone who comes from a point west of Thirlmere if you hope to settle peacefully here, Mr. Gamble," I rallied him.

"I expect they'll be calling me a demmed soft easterner, next time I go home to visit. I'm glad you have not taken into your head to be offended with my offer. I meant no harm, I assure you."

I muttered some sound of approbation. His glass was about empty, raising a hope he would take his leave. I had done all that politeness demanded, and a good deal more than I ever expected I would. He did nothing of the sort, but crossed one leg over the other, hinted outrageously for a refill, and settled in for a neighbourly chat.

"It is unfortunate that we should be virtual strangers, Miss Barwick, particularly when we will soon have something in common. I refer to my new career as a sheep farmer. Where would you recommend I apply for fellside for grazing? Heaf, we called it in the west."

"We speak the same language here in the east. We are not such total strangers as that."

"Since Leroy sold his flock and Chapman is turning brewmaster, I might get the fellside between their two driftroads. I expect part of the herds might be up for sale next auction. Wingdale, I believe, is the gent who presently holds them."

"I wish you luck of getting anything from *him*, Mr. Gamble."

"Folks call me Jack," he mentioned. "Yes, I know nothing will come at a bargain from Wingdale. What do you think of his notion of turning the place into a tourist mecca?"

"It would be a *desecration!*" I said.

"We had better put a spoke in his wheel then. Do others share your view?"

I was ecstatic to see he shared my view, for though I found much to dislike in the man, there was no denying he was the most influential person in the neighbourhood, or soon would be. "Certainly they do!" I assured him.

"Why do they go on selling to him then?"

I had so long carried my disgust and fear of Wingdale in my bosom that it erupted like a volcano. All my suspicions were aired—the barn burnings, and more recently the accidents to the wall and Scout on our own heaf.

"This should be reported to the authorities," he said, greatly surprised that it never had been.

"Much good it would do. Wingdale *is* the authority. It is no secret he runs Grasmere."

"That will come as news to my uncle. He is still the Deputy Lieutenant for the district of Westmoreland."

"He has taken no active interest for a few years. It is Wingdale who has appropriated the function of appointing the magistrates locally, including himself. He has put himself in charge of the militia group we have here. It must have been done with your uncle's agreement." It had not occurred to me before, but once it entered my head, I began to wonder whether Wingdale had not paid the old earl some sum to acquire these prerequisites.

"I wonder..." Gamble said, then stopped, leaving me hanging in a limbo of curiosity. "That would explain the old boy's having been able to obtain such staggering mortgages. I wondered that anyone would give him such huge ones. Anything above seventy-five percent is generally impossible to obtain. The Hall is mortgaged to the tune of...well you would not be interested in that," he said, very erroneously.

"Pay the mortgages off if you can, Mr. Gamble. Wingdale has some way of buying them from the bank and foreclosing at the first sign of non-payment. It is another of his tricks for stealing properties. I have wondered from time to time if he had not his eye on the Hall, as the star of his new village."

A grim, mocking smile alit on Gamble's swarthy countenance. "This promises to be a more interesting fight than I thought. I have taken up more than enough of your time, Miss Barwick. I must return home."

"Is Lady Irene still with you?" I remembered to ask, before he left.

"She went home to replenish her wardrobe, but has promised to return to us soon."

"How is Emily?"

"Blooming. Since I have been taking her about a little, she has turned into a butterfly. Now she is after me to take her dancing again tonight. Would you care to join us?" he asked.

I had never been more in charity with Gamble than I was at that moment. For that reason I hesitated, though I feared the dancing would occur at Wingdale Hause. "Where..."

"Wingdale's. I know you dislike the spot, but it will give us an excellent opportunity to observe The Enemy," he said, smiling in a conspiratorial way. "*Do* come," he urged.

I sat wavering on the edge of acceptance, wanting to go, yet not wanting to break my word to myself. "Or would Mr. Carrick take it amiss that I ask you?" he added, with a hesitant expression. "I shall invite him to join us, if you wish."

"No!" The word was out, loud, firm, almost horrified, before I thought what I was about. "He is busy," I said, and I am pretty sure I blushed.

His face split into a grin. "Ah good, then it should not be necessary for you to have any headaches. This has been a very informative visit. We shall call for you—just Emily and myself—at eight. All right?"

"I don't know," I replied, and felt perfectly asinine to hesitate so long over a minor engagement.

"Live life, Miss Barwick. You work hard and deserve to play hard too. It is the only way to live. Believe me. We shall come for you at eight. If your conscience gives you too hard a time, you can stay home. Ambledown is practically on our way, so it is no inconvenience, but I hope you will come."

At last he left, walking back across the meadow, to return home via the fells. I should have offered to loan him a mount, or a carriage. Instead I sat wondering what to do. All the day long I continued wondering as I went about my business, contacting the fence menders and finally sending the groom over to Ritson's place to buy Becky, asking him to bring home a bill, to be paid by some as yet unknown means. My heart was light, considering the unpleasant nature of my day. I was by no means too tired to go dancing at night. The idea was very appealing somehow, if only Wingdale Hause were not the spot chosen.

= 10 =

YOU SHOULD ALWAYS stick by your conscience. You *know* when you have made the right decision. I was correct in having vowed to stay away from the assemblies at Wingdale Hause. What a price I paid for giving in to the impulse to accompany Emily and Gamble! I had not, literally, a single moment's enjoyment from beginning to end. It was a chaperone they wanted, nothing else. Hennie, in an effort to ingratiate herself with the old earl and perhaps pick up some bauble in his will, had taken on the duty of sitting with him in the evening. My bad temper may lead me to do the woman an injustice here. It may have been her taste that steered her away from the assembly. My main displeasure in the evening, however, was not wounded vanity at being used as a chaperone.

I was put in a pucker from the start when the first person I saw there, dancing with all the local cits' daughters and tourists, was Tom Carrick. To be sure he never told me he did *not* attend the assemblies, but I took his nodding approval of my oft-repeated opinion to mean he followed the same course. It was not his dancing that annoyed me so much as his mere presence, after I had told Gamble he was busy. You will be thinking it served me well, and so it did, but that element only exacerbated the offence. Of course, he dashed right up to us, making such a pest of himself for an hour, despite my frostiest manner, that we provided a very amusing spectacle for the onlookers. It seemed to me all of genteel Grasmere was there, all of it between, say, eighteen and forty. How they could waste their time, coming here night after night!

And the way Wingdale had got the place rigged up was a joke. Whether it was his life on a crowded ship or economy of space that accounted for the chairs and tables being on top of each other I know not, but I know every time anyone wished to get to the dance floor he had to slither like a snake between the minute spaces left for passage. His notions of opulence and gracious living must have been picked up at Bartholomew Fair. There was a circus atmosphere about the place—everything too bright and gaudy. Any corners of the walls that had escaped gilt were draped with shimmering satin (some bright red, some bright blue). He had fresh cut flowers on every table—not a token bouquet but a crystal vase a foot high, with two more feet of blooms sticking out the top, making it impossible to see half of one's party. Every youngster in town had been stuck into a little red jacket to play waiter, hustling wine to the tables before a bottle was half empty. I would like to have got a look at the bill for this evening's farce. Whatever the cost, his patrons seemed to feel it was worth the price. The noise of laughing and talking did a fair job of overwhelming the music.

Jack Gamble took the ill-conceived idea of asking Tom to join our table, so that he would not have to take any part in bearing me company himself. He (Jack) danced first with Emily, then with anything in a skirt that would have him. The local milliner enjoyed a half hour of his company, as did the doctor's wife and the parish officer's sister. A tourist in a corner being called Lady Trevithick occupied a good part of his evening, first in wangling an introduction to her and later in paying her court. Between dances he wiggled his way between the tight tables back to us, to laugh at Tom and me. If he said one word about headaches, I would have lifted the decanter and hit him on the head with it. After I had six times refused to stand up with Tom and be squeezed to death on the floor, he took into a snit and stood up with Cora Mandrel. I shall mention in passing that she was the lady who had enjoyed his attentions before he took to annoying me with them. She is short, blonde, not outrageously ugly, and rich. Her father owns a large piece of Manchester, they say.

When Tom went from Cora to her married sister, Lisa Blackmore, Gamble took pity on me and asked me to join him for a country dance. A country dance, if you please! You would take your life in your hands to venture on that crowded floor for a well-ordered cotillion or minuet, let alone a country dance. I gave him my opinion of that idea in no uncertain terms—in the dead of summer, too, in an unaired hall. The heat was one of the more outstanding aspects of the place, and I had not thought to bring a fan either. The perspiration stood out on my brow. Gamble, hoping to prevent my suggesting we go home, took up a menu from the table and began fanning me, causing the neighbours to smirk and whisper, before following his lead and fanning their own ladies. "I shall be your punkah wielder," he declared.

"I expect *you* are quite comfortable in this stifling place," I said.

"No, I am never *quite* comfortable when a lady is so high in the boughs as you are this evening. Pray, if the question is not impertinent, why did you come if your intention was only to sit on the sidelines scowling at everything and everyone?"

"How was I to know it would be a hundred degrees?" I asked querulously.

"It would be as hot at home, with nothing to divert your attention. I believe you are angry that Carrick came, after telling you he was busy, but if that is the case, sulking won't bring him round. You must show him how little you care that he..."

"How *dare* you suggest ... Oh this is too much!" I said, flinging his menu aside and making as though to arise.

"Suggest? It was you who told me so."

"Why did you ask me to come here anyway?" I demanded.

"I have just been asking myself the same question," he said, and looked around the room, selecting his next companion. He had waited too long to join the country dance and was obliged to sit with me, making very desultory conversation—and drinking a good deal of wine. As the next set was about to begin, he nodded to Captain Wingdale, which brought that hateful person darting to us. This nasty trick accomplished, he said, "I leave you to make your compliments to the Captain for the de-

lightful evening he is providing us, Miss Barwick," and left, to
return to Lady Trevithick's table. That table consisted of three
ladies and one gentleman. The females would have looked more
at home at Covent Garden than St. James's, despite the borrow-
ing of a title by one of them.

"I am happy you have deigned to come amongst us at last,"
Wingdale began, with an ingratiating bow, as he lifted his coat
tails and slid on to the chair beside me.

My first aim was to undeceive him as to the idea that I was
enjoying any delightful evening. "How warm it is," I said,
picking up the menu to fan myself.

"An understatement," he allowed. "It is deuced hot. Hotter
than the hobs of...Hades."

"Odd that people choose to dance in such weather, is it not?"

"Aye, so it is, but it is very good for the sale of beverages,"
the merchant informed me. "You are not drinking, Miss Barwick. Allow me to order you a glass of wine. On the house—in
honour of your maiden visit."

"No, thank you," I said promptly. I received not only a glass
but a whole bottle of champagne, delivered with great pomp
and circumstance by a parade of three red-jacketed boys, so that
the entire room stared in my direction. I, who had been shout-
ing from the roof tops for months that I would never darken
Wingdale's door, was forced to sit and accept this unwanted
hospitality.

The evening continued its decline from execrable to intolerable. Tom took to flirting so noticeably with Cora Mandrel (I
think really he was a little tipsy) that there was no point pretending he cared a fig for me. Gamble, smiling slyly from the
other side of the crystal vase, looked from Tom to me half a
dozen times. When at length Captain Wingdale asked me to
stand up with him, I accepted! It hardly mattered; my credi-
bility was utterly sunk already.

I feared some heavy-handed gallantry from the man but was
surprised. His aim was to talk business, in the middle of a
dance. "When will your brother be home?" he asked.

Taking it for mere chit chat, I said only that he would be back soon.

"You are having a difficult time of it without him," he said, in a sympathetic way.

"My brother has never taken much interest in the farm," I condescended to tell him.

"No doubt that is why it is in such a shocking state."

"I beg your pardon?"

"No offence, ma'am. No offence intended. But you know I take a great interest in that stretch of country near Wingdale. I have my eye on you," he said jokingly. Oh, but there was truth under the little sally. "Things cannot go on much longer in such a state. I'll tell you, Miss Barwick, I am ready to talk business any time you are."

"I am not ready to talk business at an assembly, sir!" I declared haughtily.

"We both know I don't get many chances to talk to you. Now be sensible, do. A lady cannot run a sheep farm, and your brother don't want to. If you're wise, you'll sell up while the place is still worth something. Another year of sinking deeper into debt, and a sale won't bring enough to break even. I want the land, those acres between your house and Barwick Pike behind. I'll tell you what I'll do, Miss Barwick."

"Captain Wingdale, I do not wish to discuss it."

The steps of the dance (a cotillion it was) determined that we separate. No sooner had he twirled back within ear shot than he was at it again. "Here's the bargain, and no money changes hands at all. You give me your holding—keep the heaf if you like, it is of no use to me—turn over your house and lands, and in exchange you and your family get one of my tidy new cottages. All the extras and luxuries you could want. More than you have now."

I accepted Mr. Gregory's hand, with a glare over my shoulder at the merchant. When we met again I was still glaring, and he was still bargaining. "Throw in a fence around your place, an *iron* fence, and space in the back for a garden. The other cottages won't have half so fine a place. Only right the Barwicks have some extra distinction. One of the finest old families in the district.''

"No!"

"And a closed stove," he tossed back at me, as he advanced to his next partner and to the next step of the dance.

That is how the dance proceeded till its termination. A carpet for the stairs and a years' free subscription to the assemblies here at Wingdale Hause were thrown in before it was over. I was still saying no.

"She's a hard bargainer," he said to Gamble when he brought me back to our table. Then he spoke to me, in a low voice. "If you're wise, you'll accept my terms, Miss Barwick. There's more than one way to skin a cat."

"You'll find Ambledown does not burn easily, Captain!" I shot back, in a voice a few notches louder than his own.

He flashed a dangerous glance at me, clamped his common lips tight, and walked away, straight-backed, fast, angry.

"Mr. Gamble, I wish to go home now," I said, with my chin in the air, and possibly a dangerous sparkle in my own eyes. Jack gave me no argument but offered his arm to Emily, and the three of us strode out the door. Wingdale did not come to make his adieux, as I half feared. Neither did Tom, but I don't think he saw us go.

"What happened?" Gamble asked, as we waited for the carriage to be brought round.

"Wingdale wants to buy Ambledown, to tear it down and throw up eight or ten cottages in the meadow."

"What price did he offer?"

"He is not so fast as *you*, sir. He didn't actually name a figure."

"I take it you're not willing to sell?"

"I cannot sell my brother's estate, and would not if I could."

"Might not be a bad thing," the unfeeling creature said, very offhandedly. "What I mean is, it is a shame to see the place go to rack and ruin. If Edward cannot keep it up, it would be well to see it in the hands of some caring family who would do so, but I do not mean Wingdale, obviously. Its historical associations add some charm to the district."

There was very little conversation as we went home. Emily made some yawning remarks about the assembly. Just before I was left off at the door, Jack said, "If Edward *does* sell, I would like to arrange to purchase his heaf. Wingdale won't want it, and I need feeding acreage for the herd I am purchasing."

"You must get together with Wingdale and help him set a torch to the place then, as he implied he meant to do."

"You can't mean he said that!"

"Not in so many words. It was a veiled threat, but if we have any more broken fences, killed dogs, or *particularly* any fires, I mean to bring in the authorities from outside the parish, if the local ones do not act. In fact, it seems to me it should be reported to someone that our Deputy Lieutenant is inactive, and has sold his prerogative to maintain law and order to a felon."

"That is dangerous talk, milady."

"The Captain is not the only one who can threaten. As he is such a great and good friend of yours, you may feel free to tell him what I have said."

"I have overestimated your intelligence," he said with a weary sigh. "I might have known a *woman* . . ."

"I am intelligent enough to wish I had stayed home, in any case."

"And foolish enough to have forgotten why you went. This was our opportunity to feel out the enemy, remember?"

"It seems to me I learned a good deal more from him than *you* did. I cannot think the female calling herself *Lady* Trevithick, who is a mere tourist, provided you with any useful clues in the matter."

"Oh but she did! Only the tourists know what the tourists want. Wingdale is not providing anything to the higher class tourist—those who wish to blend a little culture with their entertainment."

"I think he is providing the sort of culture *she* wants. And in any case, we are not in the business of entertaining tourists. My own wish is to be rid of them."

"You can't turn the calendar back. Our little paradise here amidst the lakes has been discovered by the world. Someone is going to exploit it—the Wingdales, or someone with better taste."

"You sound as if you plan to join in the activity."

"Hurry up, John. I'm tired," Emily called from the carriage.

"Sorry you did not enjoy your evening," he said, bowed, and left.

== 11 ==

WITH SO MUCH on my mind, sleep proved impossible. At three o'clock I went downstairs to sit on the front porch in my nightgown and not a stitch else, it was so hot. It was so oppressively muggy I wished I had one of those punkah wielders Gamble had spoken of. The moon hung low in the sky, a fuzzy moon, due to the haze and moisture in the air. No stars were visible. A little breeze was blowing up from the lake, enough to cause an impression at least of coolness. I sat alone in the darkness thinking, plotting to discover a path out of our financial difficulty. If I paid the fence menders and Ritson (for Becky), our mortgage could not be met. The bank had extended it before, but I did not like to ask it at this time. They might use it as an excuse to sell it to Wingdale, who would certainly foreclose. I was sure he had arranged the trouble with our walls and Scout's death— had done it to force us to renege on the mortgage payment.

It was a difficult decision to make, but at about four in the morning it was suddenly very clear. It was inevitable. I must sell my dowry, and use the proceeds to pay our bills. I do not refer to anything so grand as money when I speak of my dowry. It consists of a little jewelry, a silver tea service, and some plate left me by my mother . . . With the tourists coming to town, there was a good market for such items. The tea service, for example, would fetch a fair price, enough to pay for the wall and Becky. The other things would go, too, in bits and pieces. And then what was left to sell? Myself. I would marry Tom in the end, very likely, but not without a good fight first for my freedom.

It was extremely unpleasant, having to sell this part of my

heritage. Not the least humiliating was to see the treasured items sitting in the window of the used articles shop not ten minutes after the bargain was struck with Oldham, the proprietor. They would be recognized by the tabbies of Grasmere, the fact of their having been sold discussed over tea. Never mind, they were not the first local silver to decorate Oldham's window, and they would not be the last.

The sale had one unforeseen consequence, whether for good or ill I do not know, but I know it was very distressing. I sold the set at eleven in the morning, deposited the money in the bank against the bills soon to be coming in, and went home quickly to Ambledown to mourn their loss. It was not much later than half after two when Tom's carriage came rattling up the road. When he alit, he carried not his customary meal but a large carton. I was angry with him after the preceding evening's performance. Not entirely happy with myself either. He set the box at my feet, placed his hands on his hips in a simulation of offended anger, and said, "You might have told me, Chloe."

"What's in the box?" I asked, though I had a very good idea.

"Your tea service. Chloe, why did you not *tell* me? You know I would have been honoured to lend money—any sum you need. Within reason, I mean. You are welcome to what I have."

"Oh, Tom, I wish you had not."

"Chloe, my dear!" He sat on the chair set aside for Nora and seized my fingers in his, sending a pair of sox in the process of being darned to the grass. "It is all clear to me now. Your friendship with Gamble, your going to the assembly with him. I hope you have not borrowed much from him. I shall redeem your note at once, of course."

"I have not borrowed from Gamble! Why should I have sold the tea service if I had?" I suppose he was trying to make some sense from my sudden freakish starts.

"Thank God!" he said, weak with relief. "I own I was hurt that you should turn to him before *me*. Oh, Chloe, if I acted badly last night, that is the reason. It was jealousy, pure and simple, at seeing you there with him."

"Tom you ninny! I was acting chaperone for Emily."

"But why did you do it if..." He stopped, frowning. After a few seconds his brow cleared, as he thought he had my reason worked out. "It is because of Edward you do it. You wish to stop any gossip that Gamble and Emily are to make a match of it."

This was no new idea. I think it had more than a little to do with Gamble's having asked me, in fact. I did not mention it amidst the more exciting concerns of my evening at Wingdale Hause, but Gamble had dropped a few favourable remarks about Lady Irene. I felt his interest in Emily was waning, while his admiration for the older cousin waxed. "I was surprised to see *you* there, Tom."

"I drop in once in a while. Everyone does. It is pretty dull when one is a bachelor, you know. I would not go if...Chloe, marry me! This is nonsense, you selling your few treasures to make ends meet, when you *know* I want to marry you. Let Edward marry Emily. Your Aunt Nora can come with us or stay with them—it is all right with me, either way. Things will be arranged just as you like. And Gamble must do something for Emily if she and Edward fall into hot water. He'll look nohow if he don't."

There was some merit in his speech. It was the sane, logical way out of our dilemma. To lead him on was unconscionable. I sat debating, not finding it in my mind to refuse and not finding it in my heart to accept. In the meanwhile, the large carton at my feet posed a serious problem, for I would not accept it unless I accepted Tom too, and he had no thought of taking it home, for his mama to discover what he had done. I expressed some regret that I could not purchase it back from him.

"Keep the twenty-five pounds, and keep the silver," he insisted.

"Twenty-five pounds? Oldham only gave me twenty. Tom, we have been cheated."

"Man has to make a profit. He ain't in business for the fun of it."

"He does not have to make his profit on *us*. Fleecing the tourists provides him a very good living without robbing the local gentry into the bargain. Take it back and get your money."

"I shall do nothing of the sort."

"I am not taking that silver into the house. It is yours, and if you leave it here it will sit out in the wind and rain till someone steals it."

"Stubborn woman," he complained, but he lifted the carton from the ground back into his carriage. "It will be in my attic, waiting for you to change your mind," he warned. It was clear Tom meant to stay for dinner, and likely the evening as well. After about half an hour it became equally clear I had no intention of inviting him, so he left, once again in a fit of pique. I expect the evening would find him at Wingdale's once more, dancing with Cora Mandrel. I half wished he would offer for her, to save me the bother of coming to a decision. I'll wager she wished for it, too, for while I poke fun at Tom, he is really very nice, and eligible.

Over the next week the men got our stone walls repaired, I paid them and Ritson, Ulrich introduced Becky to her chores, Nora finished her green shawl and began a blue sofa rug, and Mr. Gamble offered marriage to Lady Emily. This latter detail came to our attention through the courtesy of Hennie Crawford. She did not often come to call on us, but she made a special trip over, with Emily in tow, to make the announcement. You could have knocked me over with a feather. I made sure Lady Irene had the inner track. They were not long seated in the saloon, the duenna reeking of onions and flexing her sausage-like fingers in her black mittens, till she puffed her breast up like a pigeon and said, "Have you heard the news from Carnforth Hall, ladies?"

There was always such a deal of news circulating about the place since Jack's return that we did not know whether she referred to the Indian pavilion under construction, the matter of Gamble's setting up as a sheep farmer, the Indian female who had given birth to a baby, or something to do with the menagerie. Before she could stun us with the announcement, Emily said shyly, "Cousin John has asked me to marry him, Chloe."

I felt a great urge to laugh. I don't know why. It was a shabby, underhanded trick for him to ask her while Edward was still away. I own it came as a shock to me, for I consider myself to be rather a dab at spotting romances, and I had been so sure this one was declining. "I hope you will be very happy," I said.

"I have not accepted yet!" she exclaimed, looking with a guilty glance to Hennie.

"She is playing hard to get," Mrs. Crawford told us. "Of course, she *will* accept, after a discreet time for consideration. It does not do to rush into things pell mell, but as I told Emily the night after John made his offer, if *she* does not have him, Lady Irene will not be long in snapping him up. She has written asking them both to spend a month with her, saying at the same time she can come to us if we cannot go to her. He is an excellent *parti*, and so very considerate. He goes to any length to please Emily. A lady would be foolish to refuse such an offer, when there is no one else of her acquaintance who can offer half or a quarter so much." This angry tirade was directed full at myself, as Edward's representative, I assume.

"Quite true. You will not do better than Mr. Gamble, Emily," I agreed, mostly to disconcert the Tartar. She did not know what to make of my agreement, and went on to point out, herself, a few of Edward's advantages, which was surely not her intention.

"Just because you have felt some attraction to Mr. Barwick, my dear, is not to think your feelings are unalterable. He is younger, of course, and his poetical nature perhaps seems more closely attuned to your own. I'm sure he is an excellent fellow in his way, but he will never be Lord Carnforth, and never possess worldly goods to match John's."

"A lady cannot overlook material considerations altogether," I agreed blandly, seeing that Emily was not at all impressed by these persuasions.

"Cousin John is so dark, almost like an Indian," she protested, becoming sulky that Edward's spokesman did not make a stronger push to attach her affection.

"Pooh, he is ten shades lighter than when he came home," Hennie averred. We had had such a hot summer he had not paled at all, though the darkening of the other males tended to make him less conspicuous.

"I shan't make up my mind till Edward gets back," she insisted.

"Don't think your cousin will wait forever," Hennie warned.

"Edward will hardly be gone that long," I pointed out. "He

is due home shortly now. I wonder Mr. Gamble did not await his return, as he knew of the affection between Emily and my brother." As I considered this naive speech, it occurred to me his wish might very well be to get her engaged to himself before Edward's return.

"He does not insist on an answer at once," Emily assured me. "He just wants me to know Edward is not the only man who wants to marry me. Perhaps you will tell him so, Chloe."

I was fast falling out of charity with the minx. She would not have had an offer from Gamble without some encouragement on her own part. Of that I am certain. He is a proud man, one who would not enjoy being rejected, especially by a chit scarcely out of the schoolroom. It looked wonderfully as though her only reason for encouraging him was to work Edward up to an offer. Seventeen years old, and she knew every trick in the book where men were concerned.

"I imagine you will tell him yourself, Emily," I answered curtly.

"I will if he calls," she admitted frankly, her face the picture of innocence. She plainly saw nothing wrong in using all her wiles to win a husband, *the* husband of her choice.

Hennie sat on for some time, puffing up Gamble's merits to his cousin. It occurred to me she would welcome a cup of tea on this occasion. She was not offered one, as our silver tea service was in Tom's attic, and I had no intention of pouring from a china pot with a chipped spout. She took very well to this snub, as some strange people do, mistaking rudeness for breeding. Before she herded Emily out the door, she said, "We look forward to seeing you soon at Carnforth Hall, ladies. You must come and see all the innovations Mr. Gamble has initiated."

"How fare the elephant and tiger?" I asked.

"You are very interested in wild animals, are you not, Miss Barwick? He speaks of sending them to Exeter Exchange, for there is no denying they are a nuisance. At least he said he would offer them to the Prince of Wales while he is in London."

"In London? We heard nothing of that!" Nora exclaimed.

"Why yes, he left a few days ago, just after he proposed to

Emily. We are very dull without him. He is hiring a house for next season, you know," she said, looking to see how Emily reacted to this future treat. "So you will come and see us soon?"

"Yes, we'll come," I said. I was as curious as anyone else would be to get a first-hand look at the freak show, and preferred to do it while Gamble was away.

== 12 ==

WITH SO MANY souvenirs from India in evidence at the Hall, folks were beginning to refer to it jokingly as Calcutta Hall, or any other Oriental-sounding name they could invent. I was itching to get up to see it for myself, and intended going the very next day. What must happen but Nora came down with a bout of influenza. Not another soul in the whole neighbourhood was so afflicted, and not another soul affected my own life so much as Nora. Naturally I could not dart up to the Hall and leave her unattended but for the servants. A week passed before we were able to go. It was probably the longest week of my life. Word was out about Nora's illness, keeping callers away in droves. Nor could I be sure of any warm welcome in the village, so I stayed home, with not even Edward for company in the evenings.

The trip to the Hall was therefore a particular treat for me, when the great day came. Already the exterior of the place showed the improving hand of Gamble. The meadow had been cleared, windows glistened in the sun—some order had been reestablished. The greater change had taken place inside. Someone—I suspect Hennie Crawford of the deed—had taken the household management into hand. Surfaces once invisible for dust and debris now gleamed, the sheen of mahogany undimmed by opaque windows. The gray tatters had been stripped away to be replaced by lengths of sea-green brocade, valanced across the top. White sheer underhangings created a feeling of softness at the mullioned windows. I yearned to try this extravagant trick at home. Underfoot, new carpets stretched, the nap on them unmarred by more than a week's traffic. The blackish-green silver had been polished till it winked in the sun.

So far so good; all commendable improvements. But cluttered in amongst the English silver and mahogany traces of India obtruded, causing a jarring note to the whole. An ugly gray tub in a corner that held periodicals, for instance, turned out to be made from an elephant's foot, monstrous toenails still intact. A truly bizarre metal piece with what strangely resembled a snake attached to it was described as "Cousin John's hookah." This oddity was for smoking, but smoking of no type ever seen in England. There was water involved, and even perfume, I think Hennie said. Inlaid tables too small for anything but holding the bits of carved ivory and brass bibelots were stuck at random about the room's edge. Bright, not to say *garish*, throws littered many a sofa and table. They were pieces of Indian weaving. *One* might have added some interest to the room. The seven I counted in a cursory tally were definitely too much. One rather expected to see customers roaming through this bazaar.

Hennie looked to us for approval. "I am planning to surprise Cousin John when he returns," she told us. I began to wonder if this was why we had been asked up, to admire her handiwork. There is no denying an artist wants a few claps after finishing a project. Nora's first move when she ties the last knot in her netting is to shake the piece out for my admiration, then she bundles it up to take to show off to her cronies in the village. The sparkle in Hennie's eye and the fatuous smile on her lips told me she was vastly impressed with her own ability, and now wished to hear it praised.

"Lovely. Charming. So original—quite unique," I said, my eyes running from corner to corner, discovering another curiosity at every turn.

"This is certainly an improvement from the last time we were here," Nora said, with real feeling. This opinion I could second with no qualms. Nearly anything was preferable to the incredible filth and confusion of the last visit.

99

Then the parade began. Lord Simian led it. Emily's monkey came swinging in to greet us, hanging by one paw from the top of the door frame. He was outfitted in a green velvet jacket and yellow trousers, looking like a little miniature footman for our tinker's wagon. The imp had better manners than some of the inhabitants of the place. He came to shake our hands at least. I don't suppose he meant any harm when he subsequently tipped over a vase of flowers, and in any case, it was only water he spilt on the carpet. One would think it were ink at least to see Hennie splutter. Emily got a hand on the animal, holding him on her lap like a baby while she stroked his head. Lord Simian liked this attention very much and showed his appreciation by smiling up at her at frequent intervals in the most comical way. Hennie hollered for a servant to come and clean up the mess. Not one, not two, but three white-clad Indians pattered in, every one of them incapable of comprehending English. She pointed, she gesticulated, she shouted louder and louder, and finally ran to get a cloth to mop up the spill herself. With her face red from frustration and exertion she explained, "I am trying to teach them English. They perform very well when John is here. It is this crew that cleaned the windows for us. They are really very good workers, if only they understood what is wanted."

"That does make it difficult," I sympathized.

"Would you like to see the elephant and tiger, as you are always talking about them, Chloe?" Emily asked.

"I would like it very much."

Lord Simian appeared to speak English better than the servants, or at least to understand it. He hopped up and grabbed me by the hand, to lead me directly to the menagerie. Gamble had had a ring erected back of the stables, where the tiger and elephant wandered—not together, but as I got closer I could see there was a high fence between them. What a great deal of trouble and expense he had gone to, fetching these wild beasts all the way home from India, only to lock them up in a little pen. What an impulsive, extravagant streak he had in him.

You are familiar with the stench of stables and pig sties. Multiply it by a factor of two or three and you will have some approximation of what assailed our nostrils. The poor tiger paced, desolate and alone, in his pen. The elephant was infinitely bored. He brightened a little when Lord Simian hopped aloft his head, but it was only a lagging ride the poor monkey enjoyed. There were more of the white-clad (closer to gray, due to their duties) servants about, carrying water and ensuring that the beasts did not escape. One trembled to think the damage that tiger would do to a flock of sheep, when a skunk can make such inroads. This whole project struck me as an exercise in futility, but I had never seen either a tiger or an elephant before, and was interested to watch them a moment. I made no demur when Nora suggested, after a quick glance, that we return indoors.

Hennie was awaiting us. She had prepared a tea that closely resembled a banquet, till one got closer to the intriguing platters to find they contained sweets of sticky, gooey, totally inedible stuff concocted by the Indian servants. The bread and butter were unexceptionable. When we had eaten not our fill, but what was edible on the table, Hennie turned to Emily. "Why do you not run up to your papa, my dear?" she asked. Some scheming light in her eye warned me this was an excuse to be rid of the girl. I waited in eager anticipation to hear what she would say.

"Sweet child," she said, smiling after her. "A lovely, well-dispositioned girl, but no manager. You would not credit, Mrs. Whitmore, the state of the Hall when I arrived. I fear little Emily will never be a manager, or a worker." She nodded sagely on this phrase.

"You are to be congratulated," Nora said.

"One is always happy to lend a hand. Poor Emily—so inadequate to run a house. Even a *small* household," she added, meaning an Ambledown-sized household, you see. She was telling us what a poor wife she would make Edward.

"So much worse for a *large* household," I pointed out, in a tone similar to her own.

"Very true. She never could manage Carnforth Hall alone," she agreed at once, to my initial astonishment, till I took in "alone." Poor Emily, she had no chance of being alone. Hennie meant to stick like glue, but I did not wish her to see how quickly I read her mind.

"I cannot think that even half a hundred servants who speak no English will be of much help."

"I am a widow—I would be able to come to her without too much inconvenience. I live alone, but for my servants."

There would be no coming to her; the woman had no intention of ever leaving. She wanted a luxurious, free home, to be virtually mistress of Carnforth Hall, and meant to obtain her goal by marrying Emily to John Gamble. Lady Irene would be no use to her. She would take the reins in hand herself. Those green curtains in the room we sat in told that clearly enough.

"Mr. Gamble has made his offer. We must wait now and see whether Emily decides to have him," I said, in a tone that told her I was terminating this topic.

She pressed her point no further, but went on to tell us of a hitherto unrevealed streak of wastefulness in Emily, which eventually worked round to her lack of dowry. Nothing was omitted to show us how totally ineligible she was for Edward yet so perfectly suited for Gamble, who appeared to like wastefulness very well, if I understood the woman aright.

I had had enough, and as Nora had run out of wool, she expressed no interest in lingering. When we arose to go, Hennie suggested we go above to say good day to Lord Carnforth. This sounded a perilous enough notion to me, but when we got there he was more or less sober. He was in a foul mood, however, so that we did no more than say good day, compliment him on his improved health, and leave. There was no sign at all of Emily. I should think she was hiding in her room to make Hennie think she was visiting her papa. We returned below before Hennie expected us. She was not waiting for us. A brown-skinned female servant was there, dusting furiously at the bannister with a feather duster. Repeated requests to her to call Mrs. Crawford did no good, no matter how loudly we asked her. She left but did not bring our hostess.

While we stood wondering how we were to get home without causing offence and without waiting an hour, there was a sound of a new arrival outside. Mrs. Crawford was drawn to the hallway by the noise, which proved to be caused by Jack, returned from London. I was mortified to be caught snooping around his house during his absence, for that was precisely my reason for being there. I had not thought he could have got to London and back so fast.

He greeted us very cordially, but his first interest was to ask for Emily. She had either heard his approach or figured she had visited long enough with her papa to satisfy Hennie, for she came down the stairs just then. I was bristling with curiosity to see how the two greeted each other, but with so lively an audience they did no more than exchange a kiss on the cheek. He then invited us to have a glass of wine with him.

"We have just had tea," I answered.

"Stay a minute," he said, and took my arm to lead me back into the saloon. Emily was a step ahead of us. He never took his eyes off her till we got to the doorway. There he stopped and looked around from object to object with a startled face, showing any pleasure only at his new draperies.

"You *have* been busy, Hennie," he said, in a strange voice. Seeing that she was smiling in anticipation of congratulations, he added, "It looks lovely. Lovely." The last word sounded lost.

We all trouped back in and sat down, Nora and myself feeling the letdown, the anti-climactic sensation of returning to a place you wished to leave. "Did you have any luck, John?" Hennie asked with no preamble to indicate what she referred to.

"Excellent luck. Things promise to go smoothly."

I imagine my curiosity was sticking out all over me. Mr. Gamble took pity on it and explained his business. "When a gentleman comes back from India, you know, ladies, his first item of business is to get himself elected to the Board of Directors of the East India Company, to have a say in affairs there."

"I did not refer to *that*, John," Hennie began. A silent, rebuking glare from Gamble quieted her very effectively, kindling my curiosity to a raging flame.

"You refer to the menagerie," he said, obviously substituting another item for that to which she referred. "You will be happy to hear, Hennie, that Prinney was delighted with the offer of our beasts. He has been wanting a new elephant, since his has become so sluggish he does not remove the visitors' hats with his customary relish. Of course, the female tiger was brought home at the request of the manager of the menagerie, in hopes of breeding her with their male.''

We had a glass of wine, then Gamble arose and began to pace the room, snatching unhappy peeks at all Hennie's artistic endeavours. "My legs want stretching after sitting in the carriage for hours," he said. "Ladies, would you like to come out and see the animals we were just speaking of?"

"We have had the pleasure," I answered, drawing out my handkerchief and putting it delicately to my nose. The aroma of the menagerie lingered in its fold. I quickly put it away again.

"Have you seen the pavilion?" he asked.

"No, we forgot it!" I exclaimed. It was one of my main interests, but Hennie's plottings had driven it from my mind.

"Would you like to see it?" he asked.

"Very much!"

"It's getting late," Nora pointed out. As indeed it was, but there was no rush to get home to an empty house.

"It won't take a minute," Gamble assured her.

It was settled that Nora, still feeling a little weak, would stay with Hennie, while Emily, Gamble, and myself go to have a quick look at the pavilion.

The pavilion came into view as soon as we entered the park. Its ogee arches were topped off with a dome, not unlike the Prince Regent's Brighton pavilion. It sat at the crest of a hill, looking totally out of place in this rough, mountainous terrain.

"It does not suit the landscape at all," he admitted at once, "but it suits *me*. Reminds me of India. My servants adore it, which forms a benevolent excuse for indulging my own bad taste."

"Oh Cousin, it is not bad taste! It is beautiful, like a fairy castle!" Emily declared, her eyes shining. Her flittering attention soon turned to Lord Simian, who made an eager fourth on our outing, except that he was either tired or spoiled.

He held out his arms to be carried. The indulgent girl picked him up. As we got closer to our goal it became obvious the pavilion was far from finished. Only the framework was erected, with many men working still on the walls. About half a dozen Indians were amongst the workers. Gamble spoke to them in their own language. One was in charge of construction.

"Kari is an excellent fellow," he said when he rejoined us. "Very talented."

"He won't get many commissions in England, will he?" I asked, thinking it was a pity to waste his talents.

"This is a hobby with him. He is a linguist, a specialist in Indian literature. He will be employed with the museum in London, where they have an excellent Indian department. I arranged it during my visit to London. His family will go with him."

"I would love to go to London," Emily sighed.

"Unfortunately a gentleman cannot take a *single* lady with him on such a trip. Now if she were his *wife*, of course, not even such a high stickler as Miss Barwick would object. Would you, Miss Barwick?" he asked, turning to spare a fleeting glance to me.

"No, not even such a dragon as *I* could find fault with that course."

Emily's interest was soon diverted by the antics of Lord Simian. I could only wonder at Gamble's attachment to this child, so different from him in interest, in age, in temperament.

"When does that wandering brother of yours return?" he asked, when it was clear Emily was paying no heed to him.

"Any day now. Perhaps tomorrow."

"I suppose you wonder at my offering for Emily before his return. I *tried* to wait, but he took too demmed long. Well, he does not own her anyway, as far as that goes."

"You don't have to justify your action to me." Emily chased off a few yards after her monkey, making a little private conversation possible.

"I suppose it might seem odd to some, as she is so young. But I didn't see any lady half so pretty in London," he said, mooning after her with his eyes. I felt an urge to take him by the shoulders and shake some sense into him.

"You were looking, were you?" is all I said.

He gave a bright, quizzical little look. "A bachelor is always *looking,* ma'am. Like a spinster in that respect, I should think. When he has been stuck off in the tropics for nearly half his life, with no English women but antidotes, the looking is very pleasurable indeed. I revel in all these peaches-and-cream complexions, blonde curls. Many's the night I lay awake in the heat dreaming of cool English breezes and cool English ladies."

"The ladies' coolness does not discourage you then?"

"Not in the least. I dote on it."

"I am happy the ladies came up to your expectations. The heat of this particular summer we feel is nearly tropical."

"I am happy with both. What's Wingdale up to?" he asked suddenly, changing the subject.

"I have not seen him. My aunt has been ill, and I haven't been out much."

"I thought you looked a little peaky. I was afraid Tom was causing you more headaches," he laughed, then went pacing off to help Emily retrieve the monkey from a tree. The animal rode on his shoulder, while Emily weighted down his other arm. I did not observe much coolness in her manner, but perhaps, like the weather, he was accustomed to more warmth from females.

=== 13 ===

THERE WERE TWO unforeseen and totally unexpected develop-
ments in the near future. Closest to home, Edward returned
from his tour cured of being a poet. What a blessed relief it was!
He looked so ragged when he came in the front door I took him
for a beggar, and was about to send him out around to the
kitchen. His hair, always long, had not been trimmed since his
departure, nor had he been shaved for a few days. His jacket was
torn and dusty, and his trousers ready for the dust bin. His skin
was decorated with the remains of old bites from insects and red
welts from fresh ones. There was no talk of pellucid waters, majestic trees, or primitive rocks. He spoke of flies, midges, snakes,
and mostly of all, hunger. He had not enjoyed a good square
meal in days. The money, running low towards the end, had not
allowed of it.

He was sent to soak in a tub while Nora and I directed the
preparation of a feast to welcome the prodigal brother. His first
speech after joining us in a clean shirt was, "How do the herd go
on, Chloe? They are having a bad time of it with blow flies over
towards Thirlmere."

I would hardly have been more shocked had he enquired
about the kitchen stove, or the state of our linens. He had not
asked about his herd since coming down with Poetry Fever two
years ago.

"We have been hard hit. I had to order an extra dip."

"How many did we lose?"

"Seventeen, but the extra dipping cost us a good deal."

"It had to be done. Much trouble with foxes?"

"Ulrich says there is a pair that are keeping him on his toes."

"We'll have a fox hunt this week," he said calmly. Less and less did it sound like my brother speaking. Not a month ago all creatures great and small had been exempt from his hand.

"Scout was killed, Edward," I told him.

"Oh, lord, how did that happen? I hope you got a good replacement."

While he was in a business-like mood he heard about the stone walls, and before he left the table Nora pointed out that the silver tea service was not in its customary place on the sideboard. We did not often use it, as it was heavy and cumbersome, but it was one of life's little pleasures to look at it while we ate.

I hardly know whether Edward Repentant was more likable than Edward Poetic. "This is my fault, and I shall get it back for you, Chloe," he told me. "I think it was foolish of you to have pawned it, for those stone walls are not so important as you seem to think. They were built long ago to save the trouble of redefining the boundaries and are not so very important in keeping the herd assembled. However, it is done, and I know you meant it for the best. It's not your fault that you know so little about these matters."

We took tea in the saloon. The conversation changed with the setting. "You have not asked after Emily," I reminded him, with a nervous look towards Nora, who was already reaching into her blue rattan netting box.

"That was a madness on my part," he said, in the accents of a sheep farmer. "A madness most indiscreet. I cannot marry a penniless girl."

Nora glanced up, her eyes betraying some sorrow at losing that illustrious "Lady" for the family. I must own I was a little sorry myself. "Gamble has offered for her," Nora told him.

"An excellent match. Good for them both. Indeed it was almost inevitable, was it not?" he asked blandly.

"She has not accepted him. I think she would listen if you..." I began, then stopped. What madness was I indulging in, urging Edward into offering for her? I was becoming as foolishly romantic as my aunt, but really I *had* felt somehow that things would work out better for us all.

He directed a cool, penetrating gaze on me. "I came to my senses out on the fells, Chloe. I will never be a poet of the first rank. I have wasted two precious years of my life, time which should have been spent putting our affairs into order. I have sloughed my responsibilities off onto your willing shoulders for too long. Due to my own foolishness I am in no position to offer for Emily. Fortunately for her, she has found another to replace me. That must be my consolation. I am no longer a child, but a man ready to assume the yoke of duty, responsibility..."

I realized then something that had not been clear to me before, though I should have seen it long ago. Edward was an actor. This was a new role he was slipping into—a noble doer of duty, a shunner of life's frivolities. He was not only a man, but an old man finished with love. It was a pity he had not got the part earlier, before we sunk into such dreadful debt and hard times.

I thought his first move in the morning would be to go up to Ulrich and survey his herd. Instead, he saddled up a mount (not the tinker's wagon, his more usual mode of travel when a poet) and went into Grasmere to have his hair cut off short. He returned looking like a soldier just out of uniform. I swear his shoulders sat at a different angle, his back was more erect, while his tread was certainly firmer. Even Nora noticed that.

"I have paid the mortgage, Chloe," he told me. "I know you always worry about it." This worthy deed had been made possible by my own arranging of money to cover our other recent expenses, which he did not mention, but he was only a novice worthy after all, and deserved encouragement. I encouraged him to his heart's content.

"I also have some bad news, I fear," he said. "Your silver tea service has been sold. It is gone from Oldham's."

"I knew that, Edward. Tom bought it."

"Tom Carrick?"

"Yes, for me, but I could not accept it. And in any case, we could not have bought it if it were still in the shop. We have no spare money."

"I must arrange some funds, some operating money."

"How will you perform this miracle?" I asked, alive with curiosity. It sounded so very simple the way he said it.

"Sell off a bit of the herd. Do you know of anyone wanting sheep?"

"Mr. Gamble spoke of setting up a herd," I told him.

"Gamble! I wish it were anyone else but he! Oh never mind, it is only business after all, and at least he will pay cash. I'll go to see him."

"You really ought to see Emily too, to let her know for certain you will not be offering for her. She is awaiting your return before she gives her cousin his answer."

"Yes, I must do it," he agreed, chin up, eyes glowing nobly. Oh, he was revelling in his new role. He would enjoy the renunciation to the hilt. I was not at all sure how Emily would enjoy it.

I never did hear from Edward what she had to say, but I saw for myself the new intimacy developing between her and her cousin John Gamble. They went everywhere together—to church, to the village, driving, usually in her blue phaeton, walking and climbing over the fells. It could be but a matter of time, and not much time at that, till the announcement was made.

The second unforeseen development that followed close on the heels of Edward's return had to do with Gamble and Wingdale. They became quite the bosomest of bows. When Jack was not with Emily, he was with the Captain. If local gossip were to be believed, he took as many meals at Wingdale Hause as he took at home. More than once I saw Gamble in the yet undeveloped area to be known in the future as Wingdale. I almost began to wonder whether it would not be re-christened Carn Dale, for it seemed to me the point of all this friendship must be for Gamble to involve himself and his fortune in the business of developing the new village.

Ladies' gossip on business affairs is not always to be credited, but as Edward had now become a man of business, he was privy to what was actually going on in such important places as banks and registry offices. "Did you know Gamble has got hold of the lakeside property just below Grasmere, there on the western side of the water?'' he asked me one evening as we sat in the saloon. Edward was perusing a farming periodical, to which he now subscribed. He didn't do things by halves.

"I wish I could have a chance to give him a piece of my mind!"

"I wish you will not do that, Chloe. I am involved in business negotiations with him, you see."

"Selling him some sheep does not require the whole family to save his feelings. Did he give you a good price for them?"

"Yes, but that was not what I referred to."

"What do you mean then?" I asked, full of curiosity.

"I don't want you to worry your head about the business end of our affairs any longer. I have burdened you for too long already. This is man's work."

I felt sure it was no more than permission to graze on our heaf till Gamble got his own pasturage that was involved in this important men's business, and let it pass. It would not be long before Edward was treating me like a mindless female whose affairs were to be discussed in front of her as though she were not even present as Ulrich and his like did. Life was dull enough at Ambledown without being cut off from business. If I were to be turned into a mere domestic creature, though, I would exert myself to bring some order and if possible elegance into our home, that had deteriorated so badly. My thoughts often turned longingly to those new draperies and carpets at the Hall. How long it had been since we had afforded a new anything!

The operating money Edward had got from the sale of the sheep could not be spent on my tea service, as Tom did not come to see us these days, and I refused to allow Edward to go after him. The silver was safe in Tom's attic, whereas there were things wanting done in the barn and stables. I was not at all sorry to hear Edward planned to do them. It was pleasant to hear the banging of the hammer in those usually silent spots, to see decaying boards being replaced, and the roof mended. How I wished we might bring the carpenters to the house proper for some repairs on loose windows, sagging doors, and peeling paint, but I knew there was not enough money for these luxuries. I little thought when I so often let fall my admiration of Gamble's new carpets that Edward was hatching a surprise for me. When I returned from a meeting of the ladies charity sewing circle at Johnsons in the village, my eyes were greeted by a spanking new carpet in the saloon. It was not a cheap one either, though I would have selected some other colours than red and blue, which must bring to mind my night of horror at Wingdale Hause. When I mentally redid the room, I fancied it in gold and green, but Nora had gone with him to make the selection so I dared not utter a thing but loud praise and admiration. It was not so different in pattern from the old threadbare covering that had preceded it. In fact, I came in time to dislike it quite intensely, but I appreciated the thought, and it was better than the old.

I worried that Edward had overspent, but the closest questioning did not reveal either how many sheep he had sold, what price he had got for them, or how much all our newness cost in pounds and pence. I was no longer to be worried with a knowledge of such things; I was to worry in ignorance instead.

Edward did not speak of Emily. He was deep into his new role, strutting about his domain, smiling at the mended barn, and as the season progressed, bringing in the hay and the fruit from the orchard. He stood about on market day with the other farmers, discussing the price of mutton and the drought, good for nothing but hay, which is not all that vital a commodity in our district, where winter grazing is possible, as it is in some others. I thought he had fairly forgotten Emily, but on a Saturday in late August I went to the village with him, and we met her shopping with Hennie. They passed us with a chilly smile and a "Good day, folks," as though we were little better than strangers. There was a look on Edward's face that betokened more than a former interest.

"She was very pretty, was she not?" he said to me in a wan voice.

"She still is, Edward. She is not dead."

"She is dead to *me*," was the stoical response.

"There are plenty of pretty girls around," I said to cheer him.

"Yes, I suppose so," he agreed, without a single iota of interest.

=14=

GAMBLE WAS KNOWN to be assembling his herd from various points, becoming a fairly common sight around Grasmere, where his novelty was wearing thin. The children no longer pointed and stared when he passed by, but only stared. We saw virtually nothing of him at Ambledown because of some residual embarrassment and resentment over the Emily-Edward affair. It became my custom, in the dog days of that hot, hot summer, to take my sewing into the garden after dinner, to catch the evening breezes, and the evening antics of a pair of cardinals who cavorted in the beech trees nearby. Their sweet warble sounded so very human that I was mistaken more than once into thinking a person was approaching when they gave their first song of the evening. Strangely enough, when a gentleman came whistling up the lane I thought him a cardinal, and whistled back, in fun. I was carrying on quite a flirtation with the papa of the brood. Imagine my consternation to see Mr. Gamble come striding around the corner.

"Good evening, Miss Barwick. Is Edward at home?" he asked.

"He is visiting a neighbour, but he should be back soon."

"Good, then I shall have a chance to rest, with your kind permission?"

I nodded, happy to discover he had not realize it was I who had answered his whistle. "I am endeavouring to copy something of your pretty country garden at home," he said, looking at our tangled little jungle. "I cannot get quite the lush look of this one, somehow."

"That will require several seasons of studious neglect," I told him. After we had both looked our fill at what remained of summer splendours of sweet peas, roses, and honeysuckle, I broke the silence by asking after the ladies of Carnforth Hall, and, of course, the old earl.

"Uncle is about the same, not improved, but we have halted his decline by cutting him off the loll shrub. Not quite off entirely," he added, "but we have cut him down to a bottle a day. The ladies are fine. How do you all go on here?"

"Very well," I said, and sat wondering what subject I could introduce that would not erupt into a violent confrontation, for what weighed on my mind, of course, was his association with Wingdale, and his enclosure of the lakeside area.

"Dancing a great deal lately?" he asked, out of the blue, as it were.

My heart jerked, for I took the absurd notion that he was going to ask me to join him and Emily again, and the very memory of that evening always upset me. "I have hung up my dancing slippers," I said in a strained voice.

"Surely you are not past your dancing days yet!" he said, drawing a set of cards from his waistcoat pocket. "Invitations for you and the others," he went on, handing them to me. "We are having a ball. Emmie wants one, and if we wait much longer we will be into a year of mourning."

I thanked him, excited at the thought of so novel an entertainment as a real ball. Such heady entertainments do not come every season, or even every year, in our quiet community. I was not so excited that I failed to notice Emily had become a cozy 'Emmie,' which sounded a significant change to me. Perhaps significant enough to indicate the ball was to announce an engagement.

"Are you still manageress of Ambledown, or has Edward usurped your place?" he asked. "I know he takes considerable interest in it now, in any case. I think it is a change for the better. Not to imply *you* were an inferior manager, but solely for his own sake. Poetry is well enough as a diversion, or a career for the few extremely talented who do not have a living to earn. For such as Edward, it is a waste of precious time."

"I am happy to say he is cured of poetry. I have been put

aside completely, relegated to the household chores.''

"Now you will be free to marry and set up your own house-hold,'' he said in a casual, uninterested way, looking up at the cardinals. "I don't have any such colourful birds as these in my garden either,'' he added, in much the same way. "Pretty little things, aren't they? I wonder what's inside their heads.''

It was odd to think of that walking piece of wickedness, Black Jack Gamble, sitting in a derelict garden and smiling at the birds, but as I regarded him, I saw he was indeed happy with these simple pleasures. "You missed the English countryside while you were away, I expect.''

"Missed it? I nearly went crazy. You've no idea how desolate I felt for the first months—years really. It took years to get into the way of a totally different life. And about a month to settle back into the old. I felt *hot* this afternoon, for the first time since I came back.''

"You'll be winning the Fell Run again one of these years.''

"My youth is behind me. I think Edward could take me to-day, and *he*—well, he is still an *ex*-poet anyway,'' he finished with an apologetic smile.

"Why did you stay away so long, if you missed home?''

"It's a long way home, and a very unpleasant journey. I don't like quitting what I have started. I went to make a fortune—it took a little while.''

"What line of work were you in, Mr. Gamble?''

"I thought we had decided you would call me Jack,'' he re-minded me. "To answer your question, I shipped over with John Company—that's the East India Company—as a writer—clerk to you. I soon realized wielding a pen was not my *métier*. I made a bit of money in trading and bought into a tea plantation up north, at Darjeeling. When old Harkness, the major owner, had a couple of bad years, he sold out to me at a reasonable price. The weather improved, as did my income. I expanded into cotton—that gown you are wearing might very well have been grown on one of my plantations. I see it is Indian muslin. Once you have accumulated a bit of a fortune, other enterprises open up to you. Trading with England, and so on. My rise was not so simple or rapid as I make it sound, when you stop to consider I spent fifteen years of my life there. The best fifteen," he added in a strange voice. It was not grim, exactly, nor quite sad, though those two elements were included in it.

"You are still a young man, Jack."

"Young?" he asked, surprised. "I am thirty-five. Thirty-five," he repeated, shaking his head in wonder. "I can't afford to spend another fifteen years becoming established here at home."

This brought inevitably to mind his establishing himself as Wingdale's partner in what I considered little less than a crime. My spine stiffened—I could actually feel it. "You are automatically established here, being Carnforth's heir."

"I understand your confusion. Actually what I ought to have said is that I wish to establish the community in a manner more pleasing to me. How's that for arrogance?"

"You will soon be the equal of Captain Wingdale, changing the place to suit you. I hear you have got hold of the acres bordering the lake. If you destroy that lovely wilderness. . ." I said, then stopped in my tracks. If he did, there was nothing I or anyone could do but mourn and complain.

"What do you think of bathing machines, Chloe?" he asked, leaning back and half closing his eyes to contemplate this new modern horror. "Of the type they are using at Margate and the other ocean resorts, you know. Do you think our lake waters too cold for bathers?"

"Why not establish a permanent fair while you are about it, with jugglers and roundabouts and swinging boats, to keep the tourists perfectly happy, as you empty their pockets?"

"I'd like a touch more of quality. A miniature Vauxhall Gardens, say, with a pavilion, Indian of course, a couple of thousand of lanterns, music, dancing. . ." he rambled on, still in his ruminative pose, though I think he was peering at me through his partially closed eyes.

I could sit still no longer. I jumped to my feet, feeling a strong urge to box his ears. Instead I said, "I must go inside now. You are perfectly welcome to wait for Edward here in the garden, if you wish."

116

"Don't be an ass, Chloe," he said, reaching out with incredible speed to seize my wrist and prevent my leaving. "I have no intention of turning the place into a circus. *I* have to live here too, you know."

The pressure on my wrist was so tight as to be painful. As I wrenched free, I looked to read his expression. He was laughing at me.

It seemed a good time to change the subject of conversation. We talked without further outbreaks of ill humour for another quarter of an hour, when Edward at last appeared around the bend astride his old mare.

"Mr. Gamble, Chloe—what the deuce are you doing sitting out in the dark?" he asked.

I had not noticed it was beginning to darken. Looking towards the horizon, I saw the sun was setting in an orange-red haze that promised no rain, no relief. "Waiting for you, sluggard," Gamble answered unceremoniously. "Your sister has kindly beguiled the time away with her charming company. We haven't quite come to blows yet, but your arrival is timely."

"Come inside and have an ale," Edward offered.

"I have been gasping here the past hour, hoping she would take the hint and offer me one," Gamble replied.

"You'll never get anywhere hinting with Chloe," Edward said. "It is best just to come out and ask for what you want."

"I shall bear that advice in mind," Jack replied, looking at me in a quizzical way. He offered his arm to walk to the front door, while Edward went around to the stable.

"Oh, Chloe, I thought it was Tom with you in the garden, or I would have joined you," Nora said when we entered the saloon.

"Why, don't you *trust* me, Mrs. Whitmore?" Jack asked with a teasing smile. "Or is it only that you would have enjoyed my company?"

"Neither one!" she said, flustered. Then as she realized what she had blurted out, she went into stammering apologies till Jack blandly advised her that next time he would send for her— to protect himself. Only then did she realize he was joking, and settled down sufficiently to resume her netting.

"I see you have got a new carpet, Mrs. Whitmore," he went on, with a twinkle in his eyes there was no trusting.

"Chloe has wanted one ever since she saw how nicely you are redoing the Hall," she answered, smiling and nodding. "She is always singing the praises of your work."

"She has already complimented me on it. I have an Indian blanket that would go very well on your sofa, if you would accept it," he said, directing his speech to Nora alone. Never a glance at me.

"That would be lovely. We have noticed how the rest of the room looks shabby, with the new carpet. That is the trouble with buying anything new; it makes all the rest look so old."

"Especially when it *is* old," I said, defeated.

Edward joined us, and the two men went into his study, not deeming business suitable for the ears of ladies. They were closeted for the better part of an hour, with a second order of ale going in at the end of thirty minutes. I was on thorns for Jack to leave, that I might discover from Edward what matter was discussed.

"What on earth were you talking of for so long?" I asked as soon as we had privacy.

"A horse. Jack is selling me an excellent mount. He picked it up in London for Emily, but it is too frolicsome for her. She is frightened of it, and I have agreed to buy it."

I was disappointed, and also apprehensive. "What price did you pay for it?"

"Don't worry about the cost, Chloe. It was a bargain, and I am not to pay for it till I have the money."

"But how much? What *is* the price?"

"A fair price. Cheap, in fact," he said, and would say no more, which tended to convince me he had been rooked.

Neither did I think the purchase of a mount had taken an hour. Edward had no notion of haggling over prices. There had been more than the mount discussed, but between Nora and myself, we could not wrench it from him.

"We talked business, of course. Farming business," he admitted at last, before locking himself back up in his study, with a sly, secretive look on his face.

=== 15 ===

THE LEROY HOUSE lately sold to Wingdale was torn down, the cellar filled in, the park cleared, and ten little new excavations dug for the cottages that would replace it. Wingdale had his crews out beginning to lay the bed of a new road, straight as an arrow, as threatened. In the normal way, I would have been ill with worry and frustration, but as it happened there was an anxiety closer to home to bedevil me. Edward was running madly into debt. The mount purchased from Gamble proved to be no ordinary jade, but a beautiful piece of horseflesh that cost more than a hundred pounds certainly, though Edward would not admit it. It was the second best mount in the neighbourhood, outclassed only by Jack's own Arabian. Edward's was a Barb, a sweet goer. A horse, even such an expensive one, would hardly put us in debtors' prison, but the mount was only the beginning of his folly. Nora held me to be partly accountable, which made me feel all the worse. I had been lamenting from time to time the sad dilapidation of Ambledown, which gave my brother the corkbrained idea to call in architects—in plentiful supply at that time with the imminent building of a whole village nearby. Like the horse, they were going "cheap" (and like the horse, I think Gamble had something to do with nudging him on to it).

The house itself is built of stone two feet thick. It stands four square, solid, and will stand for several hundreds of years. The dilapidation occurs mostly at the openings, where the water has eased its way in around windows and doorframes. There the stone is perishing, and wanted replacing, as did some of the window frames and doors. There is an ornamented battlement

119

on our left facade added on by the Tudor ancestor who had delusions of grandeur. His original idea was to match it with another on the right side, but he must have run out of money for it was never built. The battlement, which is crenelated, was in some disrepair around the top. This proved to be the last straw, as far as cost went. A group of six men came and began erecting a scaffold, whose building alone took them three days. An antiquarian was called in for consultation to ensure getting all the details quite accurate, as to materials and methods of workmanship.

"Edward, we cannot *afford* it!" I moaned, more than once. It became a refrain. I was as tired of saying it as he must have been of hearing me. "I hope you have not been so foolish as to take a loan from Wingdale."

"Certainly not. He hasn't a penny to spare these days, with all his own building. I happen to know he is in a tight financial bind. Why, if it weren't for Gamble's generosity, he would have to stop construction of Wingdale."

"Gamble is footing the bill for the building?" I asked, my blood rising.

"You know he is a partner in it now, Chloe. They cannot be stopped. The whole stretch of road hereabouts is going to be built up new, and I don't mean for Ambledown to look a fright, shaming us before our neighbours. Little better than a blight on the landscape."

"Is that why you're doing this?"

"Not the only reason," he answered, flushing, but he offered no other reason.

"Where did you get the money? Tell me, Edward. Was it from Gamble?"

"Yes, he forwarded me the money."

"Oh, you fool! Don't you see what he is up to? He wants to get Ambledown away from you. They don't plan to have one old Tudor home sticking out like a sore thumb in their new village of little brick dog houses. They plan to get you over a financial barrel so you'll renege on your mortgage, then they'll snap it up and tear the house down, to stick up a dozen new ones. You must be mad to have gone along with this."

"That is not the way it is at all, Chloe. Jack *wanted* me to do the repairs. He thinks Ambledown is a lovely old historic home. Besides, I am not to pay him a penny of cash. Over the years he is to take a part of my new yield of lambs each spring."

"How large a part?"

"That has not been settled. The fact is, there is no set time when I must pay him cash, so you worry for nothing."

"Edward, you should have remained a poet. What if the flock have a low yield? How large a number are you committed to each spring? And if you cannot pay, then what? Will Gamble not expect cash instead?"

"No, he did not say so!" Edward said, but he was frowning, less confident now.

I pressed home my point. "You have not forgotten our broken walls, our murdered sheep dog—after Gamble got Ulrich drunk. Suppose Gamble and Wingdale pull some of their other stunts on us—set fire to the barn while the ewes are down for spring delivery, for example? Then what? You owe Gamble I don't know how much money, and you need not think he will wait a decade to collect, for he will not."

"He's not like that, Chloe. Not a dishonourable man."

"He stole Emily from you while your back was turned."

"That was different."

"Yes, it was worse. I should think you would have been warned by that incident."

"You never wanted me to marry her anyway."

"That's neither here nor there. You loved her, and she loved you. Had Gamble not come home, you would have married her. He stole her from you, weaned her fickle affection away with gowns and carriages and gew-gaws, and now he is stealing Ambledown from you with these unlikely loans that are never to be repaid in cash."

"You don't know what you're talking about."

"Do I not? *One* of us doesn't know what he's doing, but it is not me. I'll tell you this, Edward, I disapprove *very strongly* of your dealings with Gamble. I want nothing to do with him in future. This is your house, and if you wish to entertain the man who is determined to ruin you, that is your affair, but I shall not meet him, and I shan't go to his ball either."

"That is nonsense. We have already accepted. You and Nora are making new gowns."

"Yes, with silk and crepe bought on credit. I am sorry we ever did it."

"Well I am not," he said petulantly, and stalked from the room.

My eyes, following him, alit on the Indian blanket Gamble had sent down to Nora, which she treasured, not realizing he was only poking fun at our hideous new carpet. It decorated the sofa. I snatched it off to take to her room. I would tell her it was getting too rough a usage down here, for I could not bear to look at it another day. I regretted the purchase of extravagant silk, but I stuck to my guns about the ball. I would not attend.

I made my intention known informally to Emily a few days before the great event. She came over in her phaeton in the afternoon for a visit, tended by a groom, who never failed to accompany her now when her chaperones were otherwise occupied. With the silk bought, Nora and I went on with the sewing, planning to amaze the village with our gowns at the next public assembly, or possibly to astonish the parish at church on Sunday if we found we could not wait. If it were to be the latter, a tippet must be added to conceal the daring cut of my own. My morals must have been lowered by constant exposure to the tourists, for I would not normally have exposed so much of throat and arms, and shoulders.

Tom Carrick was also there that afternoon. He had got tired of being angry with me and came to make it up. He brought a leg of pork with him as a peace offering. I had not been able to tell him I was not going to marry him, as I had not seen him in a dog's age.

"Chloe, you are making a new gown for the ball! How pretty the shade is. May I see it?" Emily asked, not long after she was in the saloon.

"It is not for the ball, Emily. Actually, I do not plan to attend it!"

"Not attend? Why not?" she asked, blinking in disbelief.

Tom's chin dropped an inch in shock. I had not told him of my plan.

"It is a personal matter. I cannot discuss it now, but if your cousin wishes to know why, I will be happy to tell him."

She could not have cared less about this intriguing statement. "Is Edward coming?" she asked anxiously.

"Yes, he is."

"Oh, thank goodness!"

She stayed for half an hour, during which time Tom was very eager to get back to my refusal. As soon as she was out the door, he said, "I want to hear all about it, Chloe. If that fellow has insulted you. . ." His chest swelled to indicate his eagerness to defend my name.

"He hasn't. Merely I disapprove of everything he stands for—what he is doing here. He wants to live in peace in this community, Tom. If we all get together and let him know how strongly we disapprove of this development business. . ."

"Oh is that all!" Tom said. "I thought it was serious. No denying the fellow carries on with the ladies. And he all but engaged to that nice little Emily. I wonder she don't look sharp and accept him. Daresay it will be announced at the ball."

"That seems to be the consensus of opinion. Do *you* plan to attend the ball?"

"Of course I do. It would look dashed shabby not to, after I have sent in my acceptance. Besides, I have. . .that is. . .the fact is, Chloe, the Mandrels have asked me if I would give them a lift. They have a carriage but have to hire job horses, you know, and as I will be going right past their door I knew you would not mind. You will be going with Edward."

"I won't be going at all. You don't have to explain your passengers to me. Take the Mandrels anywhere you want," I said snippily. I was offended to the core. I didn't care two straws for Tom Carrick, yet I felt betrayed. Even jealous. If this dalliance with Cora grew much stronger, I would end up accepting Tom in a fit of pique.

Nora had left to take the pork to the kitchen and did not return. She smelled romance in the air at Tom's return, and wished to give it every chance to blossom. Poor Nora! I had driven her into a state of fidgets nearly as bad as my own, with my loud worrying. The upshot of her absence was that Tom grabbed my hands and grew ardent. "Chloe, my dear, it don't mean a thing! You know you are the only woman I care a fig for." It was enough to confirm in my heart my total lack of feelings for him. He persisted a little. I opened my mouth to say definitely no, but the pork was even now in the oven. He would leave at once, and it seemed uncivil to send him from the door after accepting the gift. It was a long ride home without any dinner. Such are the trivia on which our fate hangs. If I had told him...but I didn't.

He stayed for dinner, leaving soon afterwards. I went to the front door with him, hoping for a chance to tell him I had reached my decision. My act only gave him the idea I was warming to him. Edward was not so cunning as Nora. He did not stay behind, but walked with us to the door, making it impossible for either Tom or myself to say anything of the least importance. Since I had been dismissed from managing Ambledown, I had become incapable even of managing my personal affairs.

"Tom is a good chap," Edward said in the avuncular tone he sometimes used since becoming a worthy. "Jack was saying just the other day what a fine match it will be for you, Chloe. Mistress of Tarnmere. Doing pretty well for yourself."

"I'm not interested in Jack Gamble's opinion," I said curtly. How *dare* he say anything of the sort?

Edward, the gudgeon, took me at my word and turned away, forcing me to go after him to demand when Gamble had discussed me and Tom Carrick. "At Wingdale Hause today. I had lunch with them—Wingdale and Jack."

"You went to that place!"

"They serve a very tough mutton, and the price is exorbitant. Jack says when he...oh, but I wasn't supposed to mention that."

"When he is what?"

"Nothing. You asked when Jack spoke of you and Tom, and that's when it was. He said you'll smarten Tom up no end, Chloe. He thinks highly of you. You can always change the name of Tarnmere, if that is what...."

"He may go to the devil!" I said, and stormed up the stairs.

When I returned below thirty minutes later (for it was much too early to go to bed) Edward had gone out. When I asked Nora where he had gone, she said, "He mentioned something about a meeting at Wingdale Hause. It has to do with organizing the wrestling competition for next year. They feel it ought to be advertised more widely, for it would bring in a good many tourists."

"Edward is going along with that?"

"He is a very good wrestler, Chloe. Or was, before he turned poet on us. He was quite flattered at having been asked to join them. He intimated that Gamble wished to include him in running the village affairs, which pleased him no end."

"Why doesn't he just sell Ambledown and move in to the Wingdale Hause. It would save him a deal of riding."

"Now that he has such a fine mount, he does not mind the ride," she answered complacently.

As it was to be one of those evenings when every word uttered threw me into a pelter, I retired to the lamp corner with a book, only to discover that what I had picked up as a book marker was a piece of paper bearing the arms used by Wingdale at his inn. It confirmed my suspicion that his crest had been borrowed holus-bolus from Queen Anne. I do not know the technical terms employed, but it consisted of a unicorn with a leash around its neck on the right, and a lion wearing a crown on the left. There was a note scribbled on the page, a reminder of the time of tonight's meeting. The writing was not in Edward's hand, nor was it Wingdale's. As an active church worker I had seen a few of his pledges. This was executed in a more haphazard script than Wingdale's military writing. Gamble popped into my head.

I turned the sheet over mechanically, unthinking, to see a series of lines and blobs. A closer examination told me it was a rough sketch of the local area. The shape of Grasmere suggested it, while the longer finger of Windermere below confirmed my guess. I puzzled over it, for while some of the features were familiar, others were totally wrong. A curious study showed me its unfamiliarity was due to its being a map projected into the future, when Wingdale would occupy the area now containing the few scattered farms. The arrow-straight road was there, in all its splendour. It was only a rough sketch, yet for even a rough study the eye could see it was inaccurate. According to Wingdale's original plan, Ambledown was to be the culmination of his arrow street. It was not so on the map. The street not only came to us, it went shooting right through us, to terminate at Carnforth Hall, a few miles beyond. The village had been enlarged to incorporate the Hall as its highlight. Edward, lured into debt, was to lose Ambledown. It would be pulled down, and a dozen cottages put in its stead.

My blood began a slow boil, as I scrutinized the cursed map for further offences. And found them. The twenty acres stolen from village common land were checkered in with the words Pleasure Park inscribed in the haphazard script already identified as Gamble's. A half circle was drawn at the lake's edge with the words Pleasure Dome inscribed thereon. Had the map been more complete, no doubt tents for side shows would have been included.

I sat staring, working myself into a dangerous fit of rage. Could *nothing* be done to stop this curst development? The Nabob, with his pots of gold from India, meant to let this development spread out like a great stain, till he had destroyed the whole area. And how on earth could he be brought to a stop? Between them, Wingdale and Gamble had the money, the law, and half the population on their side. It would take an act of God to prevent their succeeding now.

=== 16 ===

I PASSED THE time till Edward's return by explaining to Nora the significance of my find. She was much inclined to disparage it. Only a scrap of paper after all—what did it prove? We would ask Edward what it meant when he returned. As I sat there, tallying up all the recent occurrences that bolstered my suspicions, I imagined I smelled smoke. Having failed to wrest Ambledown from us by connivance, they would burn us out, as they had the Leroys and others before them. I thought I was imagining the smoke, till Nora lifted her eyes from her work long enough to sniff the air

A sudden panic seized me. With nerves taut from imagining, I dashed into the hallway to see if the house was in flames. There was no fire, no discernable smoke, though the smell lingered here, too. There was a good wind blowing outside. I stood irresolute, wondering where to begin my more detailed search of the premises when Herbie, our backhouse boy, came pelting up the stairs.

"Fire! Fire in the stables, Miss! Come quick!"

The awful word, and the boy's strident yell, served to reduce me nearly to idiocy. We were too far removed from the village for the volunteer fire brigade to be of any use. Neither had we a large number of hands living in at Ambledown. Our help was hired seasonally as it was required for individual jobs. I felt a lurching of my heart, then a tightening followed by a brief period of nearly total unconsciousness, though I did not actually fall over. I looked into the mirror over the hall table and saw a white-faced ghost blinking back at me—wild-eyed, petrified. Then I glanced to see Herbie staring in fascination at my blanched countenance.

"Round up everyone in the house," I said, in a voice that was calm with desperation, or incomprehension. "Herbie—go into Grasmere at once and fetch Mr. Barwick—at Wingdale Hause. Take a mount—Belle."

"She's in the stable what's a-burning, Miss," he told me, not without a certain repressed glee, I am sorry to relate. Or maybe it was only shock, for he is not really a bad boy.

It was the sudden image of my beloved Belle, faithful mare and companion on so many jaunts, that galvanized me into action. I pelted out of the hallway, down to the kitchen, and out the back door towards the stables, where as yet only the west corner was alight. An orange tongue of flame licked up over the tinder-dry roof. I knew the stable was lost, but I had some hope of saving Belle and Dobbin, and the plough animals. I ran as fast as my legs could move to the big double doors and threw them open. I was well into the barn before I realized that opening the doors had set up a draught that drew the flames inward to the center of the barn. They leapt at me in a frightening way, almost as though they were human, ravenously hungry, and determined to make a meal of me. I fought back the urge to flee. There is something so elementary and terrifying about fire. But common sense told me I had time to free the animals first.

I peered into the shadows, ears cocked for their frightened whinny, worrying that panic would make them unmanageable. Dobbin, for instance, had an unstable temper that did not match his placid name. I was surprised they made so little commotion. My eyes were not yet accustomed to the darkness, where the encroaching flames gave a flickering, unsteady, and dim light. I edged closer to the stalls. They were empty but for one. Only Belle was there, snorting and frisking in fear. My fingers fumbled to find the invisible rope that closed off the end of her stall, only to feel it was already unfastened. The next step was the dangerous one. I had to ease my way in beside her to undo the rope tethering her in her stall. If she became upset, if she reared or kicked or decided to lean against me, it could be serious, possibly fatal. I was terribly aware of her large size, her great wide hips and sturdy legs. I put out a tentative hand to pat her flank, to speak soothingly in an effort to calm her, and instead I shrieked in utter terror. What I touched was not the warm, smooth side of Belle, but a human hand.

A dark shadow swam into focus before me, very close. The leaping light danced off his face as he advanced, in such a way that I could see only his eyes. What diabolic eyes they were, with the orange flames mirrored in them. My shriek had the effect of settling poor Belle into a furore. Her front legs came up. Thank God I had not gone far into the stall.

"Chloe—get out!" the shadow said. There was no mistaking that voice. No one but Jack Gamble would speak so arrogantly when caught in the very act of committing arson.

"Get out yourself, criminal!" I answered.

Belle's rear legs scuffled as her front feet reared up and came down. Her flank heaved towards me. I leaped back just in time. Before I could see or do more a blanket was thrown over my head—an evil-smelling horse blanket. What would anyone think in such circumstances? I had caught a man red-handed burning down our stable, and he meant to murder me by suffocation. My body would be left behind to be incinerated, destroying the traces of murder. My arms began flailing, my feet kicking. A strong arm was put around me, pulling me back. Jack was under the blanket too. It was absurd, but he was.

"Hold your breath, old girl. We're going through that door," he said. "Quickly now, run."

"Belle..."

"I've got her rope, and my jacket over her head. She's sound. She'll make it."

The flames made no impression on me, so thick was the blanket. We passed right through the fire, which had reached the edge of the doors on the west side due to the whipping wind. Soon we were outside, dashing farther from the flames to safety, the blanket shucked off behind us.

"Are you all right?" Gamble asked. He still had one arm around me protectively.

I yanked away and turned to give him a piece of my mind. "Yes, alive and kicking—sorry to tell you. You set that fire."

"Don't be ridiculous." He was hardly listening, but looked back to the barn to make sure the flames did their work.

"You arranged to have it set then."

"It had to be done. Sure you're all right? Better get Belle

away to safety. I had no idea she'd be left behind. Go on back to the house, Chloe."

I opened my mouth to argue. Suddenly I was alone, with Belle's rope thrust into my hands. He was gone, disappeared into the dark shadows. I ran to turn Belle into the enclosed field, where luckily Edward had left the other animals, as the weather was warm. Dobbin cantered over to greet her. I slammed the gate and dashed back to the fire, where some of our servants had gathered to stand in open-mouthed, ineffectual wonder. The horsetrough (full of water) and buckets were not even thought of as a means of extinguishing the blaze. I shouted to them to get busy, but a glance told me the futility of trying to stop so great an inferno by this means. The barn was lost, but at least it was far enough removed from the other outbuildings and the house that the blaze did not spread.

Not seeing Gamble in front of the stable, I ran around to the back, making a large circle to avoid the heat of the flames and the sparks that jumped as far, in some cases, as ten feet. Impatiently, I ran to tell the servants to come with buckets to extinguish these mini fires that were starting up in the dry grass.

By the time I reached the back of the barn there was a full-scale battle in progress. It was for all the world like a scene from the works of Hieronymus Bosch. There was an aroma of brimstone to it, caused by the flames and shadows. I did not recognize Gamble's Indian servants among the combatants at first for he had outfitted them in dark clothes on this occasion, being better concealers than their customary white. At closer range, however, their dark, thin faces and black eyes gave them away. Who they were fighting was a mystery. It was not our men from Ambledown. In fact, it was not anyone I had ever seen before in my life. It was a gang of hired ruffians, obviously, but hired by whom? Had Edward tumbled to it after all that there was trouble brewing and made this unexpected preparation? If so, I fear he had not hired sufficient men, or not well enough trained ones. Gamble's Indians had some uncanny way of overpowering them, even as they turned (the cowards) to flee. They had what appeared to be ropes weighted at the end with some object. They flung these ropes at the departing bodies, bringing them to the ground, where they would be leapt upon by one or more

Indians, and soundly beaten.

I lifted a weapon (a pitchfork left lying on the ground by a careless stablehand) and went after the arsonists, brandishing it like a herald, while I argued with myself as to the morality of actually using its sharp end, for it looked very lethal. My scruples proved unnecessary. Gamble appeared from nowhere and lifted it from my hands, as easily as taking sweets from a baby.

"Go to the house, you fool!" he raged.

This coming on top of the rest was too much. I doubled my hand into a fist and took a swing up at his chin, which he ducked. Then he reached out swiftly to grab my wrist in his fingers. Undaunted, I kicked as hard as I could at his shins, hurting my own toes a good deal more than his booted shins, I suspect.

"Hell-cat!" he said, grabbing my two arms roughly and pinning them to my sides so that I was completely helpless. Smoke, heat, anger, rage, and frustration overcame me. My eyes filled up, blurring the infernally grotesque scene before me; then the tears brimmed over and scalded down my cheeks. I felt a heave shake my chest, and an ugly, convulsive sound issued from my mouth—a groan or sob or moan of protest.

"Chloe. Chloe!" he said, looking at me, almost smiling. The night and the danger bred some madness in the air. His grip tightened. I thought he was going to kiss me. "Pull yourself together. Go to the house now. This is no spot for a lady."

"You..." I could say no more.

"We'll talk later. Go now, before you get hurt."

He dropped my arms and turned back to the fray, to become lost in the running, squirming melee of dark bodies. I did not go to the house but slunk back into the shadows, hopelessly confused and defeated, to watch alternately the collapse of the roof of the barn, and the rout of Edward's hired defenders. The Indians took the battle, rounding up two or three of the hired men, which struck me as a very odd thing for them to do. But then the whole night had been so bizarre that I did not question it. When the fighting was over and the fire no longer exciting, I walked, as one in a trance, to the house. It was empty. Absolutely, completely empty. The servants and Aunt Nora were down at the barn, of course. I sat on a chair in the saloon and cried.

— 17 —

I WAS STILL there but had stopped crying thirty minutes later when the others returned. I had succumbed to complete apathy. Edward would have to borrow more money to rebuild the barn. It would be enough to make mortgage payments impossible. Wingdale and/or Gamble would snap the mortgage up, dispossess us, and knock down Ambledown. In my mind, I saw us— Nora, Edward, and myself—walking forlornly down the road, into oblivion. This dismal prospect occupied my mind when the sound of heavy male footsteps invaded the hallway.

Edward's voice could be heard above the others. "The luckiest thing is that I decided to leave the horses out in the pasture tonight. You mentioned yesterday at lunch, Jack, that it was your custom to leave them out in summer. Maybe that is why I did it. Pity Belle was not out too, but Chloe used her this afternoon and had her stabled."

"Where *is* Chloe?" Gamble's voice asked, rather angrily, or at least impatiently.

"I expect she is..." They rounded the arch into the saloon. "Here she is, waiting for us," Nora said. The three of them looked like coal-miners. They were dishevelled and covered in soot. I realized then that I was in the same state of disarray myself. I could hardly credit Gamble had the gall to enter this household, after what he had done.

"You *arsonist*!" I charged, jumping to my feet—not without an effort, for the night had taken its toll on me.

"Chloe!" Edward said, advancing in a placating way towards me. "Jack told me of your foolish idea. You owe him an apology. If he had not been there, there is no saying Ambledown would be standing over our heads at this minute."

"Edward—don't you know what he . . ."

"Yes, yes, Chloe, I know all about it. It was not Jack who had the fire set. It was that vermin of a Wingdale."

"How did Wingdale happen to have a squad of Indians at his disposal?" I asked, with a demanding stare at the intruder.

"He didn't," Jack answered. "I brought them over. You must have noticed they were fighting Wingdale's men."

"Wingdale's men? Edward, I thought *you* had hired . . ."

"I? I hadn't a notion any of this was going to happen. It was Jack who saved us."

My conclusions were obviously wrong. To prevent making an even bigger fool of myself, I demanded to be told exactly what had happened. For sixty totally incomprehensible seconds, the three of them explained it to me. At the end of this time they realized no sense was emerging and stopped. Nora took the matter in hand. She led Gamble off to wash up. Edward, coated in grime and ashes, gave me his version of the night's proceedings, and what had led up to them.

"Jack has been suspicious of Wingdale practically from the first day he met him. He has only been pretending to play along with his plans for developing the village to learn exactly what he is up to. He worked his way into Wingdale's confidence enough to learn our place was to be included in the village—our land, I mean, while the house was knocked down. He gave me warning of it, and that is when I decided to fix up Ambledown, to make it an addition to the village instead of an eyesore. Wingdale seemed to go along with it, but when he realized how much blunt Gamble has got, he began to think of enlarging the project—stretching the village way beyond Ambledown, with his arrow-straight road, which he is so fond of, passing right through us. Wingdale learned of our financial position. He showed Jack figures to prove—well, indicate at least—that we could not possibly hang on past next spring. Imagine—you had brought us that close to ruin with your . . . Not that I mean to blame you in the least. It was and *is my* responsibility."

"We would not have been ruined! The shearing would have brought in enough to carry us, if we lived frugally."

"Aye, if our wool had ever got to market, a thing by no means certain hereabouts. I any case, Wingdale let slip something to give Jack the notion our bankruptcy was to be hastened along so that he could get on with his road and subdividing Ambledown *before* next spring, if you follow me."

"How did Gamble leap to the conclusion tonight was to be the night?"

"He thought it was suspicious when Wingdale was so very insistent that I be present at the meeting to discuss the wrestling match next year. He wanted to get me away from home, you see. Jack feels Wingdale wished to have an iron-clad alibi for himself as well. The meeting served the dual purpose of catching you ladies undefended and ensuring his own so-called innocence."

"Did you know of this before you went?"

"No, Jack didn't tell me—in case he was mistaken, you know. It would be a pretty hard thing to accuse a man of such a monstrous crime if he were actually innocent. But when Jack saw a bunch of rough-looking customers riding into town just after nightfall, he was convinced he was correct in his fears and brought his foreign servants over to catch the criminals."

"*Did* he catch them?"

"They have got four of them—not men from around these parts. They have been taken to the roundhouse. Jack thinks from their speech they are sailors, or maybe ex-sailors, which ties them to Wingdale, but they are either afraid to speak or have been well bribed to hold their tongues. We could not get a word out of them."

"This is all well and good, Edward, but I must show you what I found in your book, and the handwriting is Gamble's, not Wingdale's."

I dashed off for a piece of paper that proved Gamble's part in the planning of the village that included the destruction of Ambledown. Our heads were set together perusing the document when Gamble re-entered the room. Edward looked up, frowning at him uncertainly. "Maybe you could tell me the meaning of this, Jack," he said. His tone was markedly cooler than before.

Gamble glanced down at it. "How the devil did you get hold of this?" he asked.

"Wingdale Hause. Someone has marked on the back of it the time of tonight's meeting. The map, I notice, is in *your* handwriting."

"Yes, I drew it."

"You're quite sure the enlarged plans for the new village are entirely Wingdale's idea, Mr. Gamble?" I asked.

"Go and wash your face, Chloe," Aunt Nora said, entering the room. "You look a fright. You too, Edward."

"After Mr. Gamble has answered my question."

"You don't catch a shark with a sprat, Chloe," he answered easily, and took up a seat (an upholstered one, alas!) without regard for the state of his trousers. "I'm out to catch Wingdale. To do it, I am luring him on with grander dreams than he is capable of by himself. Wingdale is half-way to Thirlmere in his head by now, and on certain pieces of paper too. There is a menu at Wingdale Hause containing an alternative map, showing the road going around Ambledown. We were discussing possibilities, no more."

"That is very clever, Mr. Gamble," Nora said, nodding her head as though she understood his plan. I do not consider myself stupid, exactly, but I found plenty to question in his words.

"Yes, but how do you plan to catch him, Jack?" Edward asked.

"I am convinced he has committed illegal acts in the past. If the prize looks rich enough, he will do so again."

"I cannot see a development of the lakeside wilderness, for example, as being any benefit to Wingdale," I mentioned. "It was also on the map, and it is owned exclusively by yourself, is it not?"

"Yes, and he is pretty peeved he did not think of it."

"It is entirely your own idea then?"

"Just stretching his thinking a little. Feeding his greed, you might say. He has to keep pace with me, so he burned down your stable, planning to force you out, and put up more cottages. I had hoped we could definitely pin it on him, but those men have jaws of iron. We might force them to squeal yet," he added.

"You still won't have him," I said. "They'll only go up before Magistrate Muller, who is in Wingdale's pocket. There will be insufficient evidence, and the whole crew of them will get off scot free."

"Oh no, it will be carried over to Quarter Sessions at least, perhaps to Assizes," Gamble prophecied.

"Only if Magistrate Muller so decrees. He will not," I predicted.

"If any such flagrant breach of justice occurs, then the Deputy Lieutenant must intervene."

"Lord Carnforth is not much in the habit of intervening in anything that does not concern him more directly," I pointed out.

"Trust me," was his answer to that. This comprehensive order appeared to satisfy the rest of the family. I must own I was far from satisfied, but short of calling him a liar and a thief to his face, there was no way of further disputing the matter.

"The map..." I began, hoping to nudge him on to further revelations.

"He explained all that," Edward said, with an apologetic look to Gamble.

"Well, Edward, I think we have earned a glass of your excellent ale," Gamble decided.

"They will want to wash first," Nora reminded us.

When Edward and I returned to the saloon after our toilette, Nora was sufficiently at home with Gamble that she had out her netting and had as well got a towel between his trousers and the best sofa. I would have enjoyed to watch her accomplish that.

A shared incident of so unusual a nature as a fire brings forth instant camaraderie amongst the participants. Our party that evening was almost gay. Gamble assured us we were more than welcome to use his stable or barns till we had rebuilt our own. I caught on from oblique comments between him and Edward that financial help had been offered to do this. It did not seem to occur to either Nora or Edward that rebuilding would not be necessary had Mr. Gamble prevented the blaze, as he easily could have done. Had he let the arsonists see him, they would not have set the torch to our stable. Perhaps my own reticence during the evening's gaiety gave Jack some clue to my thinking. In any case, he raised the point himself.

"I limited the damage as much as possible. I hinted to Edward to leave his horses out to pasture, and had one of my own hands slip in at dinnertime to put tarpaulins over your carriages. He told me when he returned that Belle was in the stable, which is the reason you found me there, Chloe. I meant to get her out. It was my hope we could stop the blaze before it did much damage, but when the front doors were opened, the wind dragged the fire along too quickly."

"All my fault, in fact."

"All mine, you are thinking, but you are as interested in catching Wingdale as anyone. More interested than most, in fact. I felt sure you would not begrudge the expense of a barn, if it meant holding on to Ambledown."

"Yes, that is true, of course."

"We'll have a boon day and get the neighbours to raise a barn for you, Edward," he went on.

Everyone's throat was amazingly dry after the fire. Next morning I saw the week's supply of ale was gone, but I expect the servants had their full share. Cook served us some cold meat and bread, and at about two o'clock in the morning, Mr. Gamble finally took pity on us and left, allowing us to get to bed before dawn broke.

=== 18 ===

DESPITE OUR LATE night, we were up early the next morning to see in full daylight the embers that had once been a stable, and to check that Belle was unharmed after her ordeal. Two black hulks in the middle of the ashes proved to be our tarpaulin-covered carriages, the old black and our little tinker's wagon. The heat had blistered the green and yellow paint, turning it deep brown around the edges, but it was intact. A new rear left wheel was to be recommended. Edward dragged it out into the yard to be scraped.

After breakfast I went out back again to set one of our hands to this chore. He began in a peevish enough manner, resenting the tedious job on a hot morning. Who shall blame him? "Put some effort into it, or you'll be here all day," I chided him.

"The paint won't come off. It's burnt on," he grouched.

"Here, give me the scraper." I seized it, and with a few good strokes had the blistered enamel off. "There you see, there is nothing to it."

"What a versatile mistress you are, Chloe," a deep voice said, speaking over my shoulder.

I looked up into the black eyes and brown face of Jack Gamble, who had sneaked up on me without making a sound, to catch me on my knees in the dust, hair blowing in my face and hands grimed from the scraping.

"I am willing to take on most jobs," I replied, brushing the strands of hair from my face with the back of my hand.

"Everything but dancing. Is that it?" he asked, with a smile that held an edge of belligerence. "Emmie gave me your message—*finally*."

"Dancing is not usually considered a job, but a pleasant diversion. I prefer to choose my own diversions."

"And the company in which you indulge them. May I remind you Tom will be attending my ball?"

"You may if you wish, but it is not necessary. I know Tom plans to attend."

"Won't you change your mind, now that we are—friends?" he asked, speaking the last word in a tentative tone.

"As a matter of fact, I have reconsidered it." This reconsidering occurred in my bed the night before. His explanations about the village had mitigated my opinion of him to a certain extent.

"I hoped you would. Emmie's telling me you were making up a new rose gown sounded optimistic. A lady don't go to so much trouble unless she is planning to be admired by a large group. Not *this* lady at least."

"Have you come to see Edward?" I asked, ignoring his last speech. "He is at the house."

"Yes. He'll have to go into town this morning and lay charges against the culprits my thugs caught last night. I see one of them dropped his rope," he said, swinging a weighted rope from his fingers.

"Is that what they were using? It was very effective."

"Yes, it is. Come with me, and I shall show you how effective it can be."

"Come where?"

"Oh, to the nearest scarecrow. I noticed you have one in that field of grain out back. The crows are fond of it. They were pulling the stuffing out of it. Come, and I'll explain how this thing works as we go along."

He took my arm as we went out into the field, till we were about forty or fifty feet from the scarecrow. "They have a charming institution in India called thugee. Robbers strangle their victims with this device. A running noose on the end of this slip, you see. You take aim," he said, suiting the action to the word, "throw, and *voilà!*" He snapped the straw man's head off.

"Of course if the neck is held on by flesh and muscle, it only breaks. But you must not have a poor opinion of my servants.

They are not actually thugs. I taught 'em the stunt, which I learned from some of my less reputable friends in India. I thought it might be useful for shepherds, too, to return a wayward ewe to the fold. Care to try it?"

"No, thank you."

"Pretty difficult for a woman," he said, in an infuriatingly patronizing way, as he reeled in the murderous rope. Actually I was eager to give it a try. His implying it was beyond a mere female was the only goad I needed.

I reached out with a sniff for the rope. "Here, let me show you the—er, ropes," he said, lifting it from my fingers with a little laugh. He stood behind me and put his two arms around me, not loosely. My right hand was taken in his as he leaned his head down till his lips were nearly touching my cheek. "Keep calm, Chloe. You can rip my eyes out later. Now you are having a lesson," he said.

I began to wonder just what subject he was purveying. "That's enough of that!" I said, trying to pull loose from his arms.

"Tch, tch, you spinsters!" he chided, holding more tightly. "Always imagining a gent is after your virtue. I bet you look under your bed at night before you sleep, in hopes of..." he stopped short, laughing. "Really you ladies have the most salacious minds outside of India."

Any response to this charge was difficult. To let him continue was bad, to draw it to a halt after what he had just said was worse. I decided to continue with dignity, ignoring any advances on his part, unless they should be downright offensive.

"That's better, Chloe. Just stiffen up like a statue and pretend I am Edward. Or Tom," he added mischievously. There was a note of suppressed laughter in his voice. "You'll have a ripping headache by lunch time."

"What is the next step? Or dare I ask?' I demanded, deciding to make light of it. One did not wish to give him the notion she had never been in a man's arms before, though I must own I had never even been within arm's length of such a forward creature as this one.

Since we had already beheaded Jack Scarecrow, he began looking around the field for new victims, still holding me in his arms, so that we turned together from left to right, "There—you're aiming for the top of that fence post," he decided. His body stiffened, the arm went out, drawing mine with it. "Ready—go!" The rope was flung out, with little or no help from me. It missed its mark by a good foot.

"Let that be a lesson to us not to mix business and pleasure. I couldn't hit either mark. Next time you shall try it alone."

"If you think *I* derived any pleasure from this exhibition of bad behaviour, Jack Gamble, you are sorely mistaken," I declared, pushing his arm off and turning to face him.

"You are a poor loser," he commented idly, reining in the rope. "Shall I leave this toy for you? I expect you are eager to show me, after a couple of hours' practice, how well you can do it alone."

"Take it away with you. It is a stupid thing," I answered crossly, though I would not have minded to have it.

"You speak against the goddess Kali. Thugee dedicates its victims as a sacrifice to her."

"And who is Kali?"

"The goddess of epidemics, plagues, and other natural disasters in India. A witch-like deity thought to have a strong hold on ladies, especially wives. It is she who leads them to seduce their husbands and other gentlemen. Their rampant sexual cravings are thought poorly of. They threaten the gents' whole well-being."

I sought for a discreet manner in which to divert this conversation from depravity, and made the error of comparing Indian mores to English ones. "Quite the reverse of matters here at home," I said, stiff with disapproval.

"We must be living in two different worlds," he replied, widening his eyes in surprise. "*Most* of the ladies hound me to death, though I do not flatter myself my bank balance hasn't something to do with it."

I pulled my skirts around me to lessen the quantity of dust

collected, and turned to leave. He was right at my side, rattling on in the most lecherous and ill-bred way imaginable. "Sorry if I shocked you, but you ain't seven years old, Chloe."

"I hope you don't carry on like this with Emily," I said.

"No, since Hennie has come to guard her, I don't have any fun at all. That is why I have decided..."

"To honour *me* with your lecherous behaviour?"

"That's it."

"I shall go into the house and tell Edward you are here."

"I wouldn't want to put you to so much trouble. I'll go and tell him myself. I bet Nora won't be so hard to get along with," he added as an afterthought. He never loosened his tight grip on my arm for a minute, even to open the door. I felt foolish enough in front of the servants but pretended not to notice anything amiss. After he had left with Edward a servant brought me the rope used by Kali's killers, telling me Mr. Gamble told her to give it to me. She wore a sly, laughing look in her eye, but I resisted the impulse to question her. I left the rope in the front hallway so Jack would be sure to see it, and my uninterest, on his next visit.

=== 19 ===

EDWARD WAS GONE all afternoon with Jack. When they returned, we discovered they had taken lunch at Wingdale Hause. "Surely that must have been embarrassing for all of you, after last night!" I exclaimed.

"Not at all," Jack assured me. "He was quite angry about those ruffians setting torch to your barn. Well, he could hardly admit they acted on his orders. They are set to appear before Magistrate Muller as soon as someone can get him sober enough to sit on his bench without falling off. I *do* wish he would hire a new chef at his hostelry though. It is enough to make one wish for a good home-cooked meal. Is that a tatie pot I smell cooking, Mrs. Whitmore?" he asked, turning to Nora.

"Why yes, it is. Would you care to stay and try it, Mr. Gamble?"

"How very kind of you. I would indeed. I haven't had a tatie pot since I returned from the tropics—in fact, not since I left home. You must forgive my outfit," he added, looking at his day clothing.

I don't know what his motive was in inviting himself to dinner, but one effect was to make it necessary for me to absent myself from the room at once, to dart to the kitchen and oversee preparations. Bad enough that he was to sit down to a simple tatie pot, without having it served up on our everyday china. I regretted the loss of our silver tea service, which would have lent us a touch of elegance, but I had in my dowry still some fine silver serving dishes. The centre piece, an item often dispensed with when we ate *en famille*, consisted of the remnants of our flower garden.

None of us bothered to change, when our guest could not. Jack was very entertaining, regaling us with stories of India, mostly relating to food there. One story had us roaring with laughter. It involved an Indian prince who, wishing to impress his European guests with his knowledge of their customs, served them up a meal in what he considered to be their own mode, using a bedroom towel for a napkin, serving soup in a trifle dish, pudding in a soup plate, and cheese in a glass dessert dish. The champagne was poured into a china cup. The crockery was all chipped, and no two pieces alike. I was happy I had taken the trouble to have the good china put on the table and trusted Jack would not notice the chip out of the spout of the china teapot, or that the cheese was passed in a relish dish. At least the food tasted good.

Gamble and Edward played a hand of piquet after dinner while Nora netted and I played the pianoforte, softly in a corner, feeling my nose out of joint at being so ignored by everyone. The only recognition of my performance came when Mr. Gamble was taking his leave.

"Yet another accomplishment, Chloe. You never cease to surprise one. Very nice. And by the by, you will find your toy in the hallway. The rope, you know. I have seen it now, and you can take it out to the meadow to practice. If you want any more lessons..."

"I am happy you enjoyed the music."

"I am planning a tour of my lakeside wilderness tomorrow morning," he went on. "Would you care to come with me, and suggest means of developing it?"

"I do not think it ought to be developed at all."

"Ten o'clock too early?" Jack asked quickly, with a sly look at me. "Perhaps Emily and Edward would like to come along as well."

It was difficult to keep my jaw closed at this meaningful phrase. He was pitching Emily and Edward together as a *couple*, if you please, after having been at such pains to break them up. Also after having offered marriage to the girl himself. The heat of India appeared to have baked his brains, as well as his hide.

"I shall be busy arranging for the new barn," Edward excused himself, though his startled face told me he had not overlooked the mention of Emily and himself.

"I'll be by for you at ten, then, Chloe," Gamble said, speaking quickly before I could voice any objection.

"Fine, I shall go with you and Emily, if you are sure I shan't be *de trop*," I replied.

He cocked his black brows up an inch. As he went out the door, a trail of laughter wafted behind him.

When he came the next morning, Emily was not with him. I expressed my shock at her absence (a simulated shock, I confess) to be told she was not yet out of her bed, the lazy hound of a girl.

"A fine way to talk about the girl you are planning to marry!"

"You ladies aren't the only ones who can change your minds. In fact, it seems to be a characteristic of the ladies in these parts that they are unable to make them up. We gents may have to do it for you. There is Emmie leaving me dangling for months at a stretch, while you have been leading poor Tom about for some two years, as though he were a Lord Simian."

His open carriage awaited us at the front. The drive from Ambledown into that patch of wilderness by the edge of the lake is one of the prettiest in the whole country. Summer was far advanced, but it was not yet turning to yellow and brown, except in some of the fields where a second cutting of hay was about ready.

The acres annexed by Gamble were surely among the loveliest anywhere. There were clumps of trees interspersed with large patches of meadow, liberally sprinkled with the yellow and purple wildflowers of late summer. The lake shimmered beside it all. I was relieved to see the woodchoppers had done no more than clear away the dead wood. To even *think* of destroying this with some cheap pleasure park weas criminal, and so I told him.

"At present, it is enjoyed by nothing but Mrs. Cowan's gaggle of geese and an occasional cow put out to pasture. It can be more productive than that. In fact, when I gained rights of enclosure it was implicit I would farm the land. That is the whole point of enclosure, to make the land more productive, though I don't think it states it must produce agricultural produce."

"It is money you have in mind to produce here, is it?"

"And pleasure. As to the money, I have an expensive set of relations to support."

"You also have a fat bank account, brought back from India, have you not?"

"Oh yes, but my work at the Hall is putting a good dent in it. You've no idea how the old boy ran it into the ground. My expenses will be heavy, once I have established my residence in London, too. My directorship with John Company has come through. I must not be out of touch with Indian affairs, as I still have several investments there and will want a say in matters."

"Are you *moving* to London?" I asked.

"I shall have to spend several months a year there. Will you miss me, Chloe?" he asked, with a derisive smile.

"Not at all. Why should I?"

"You don't deserve any compliments, witch, but I would miss you." He straightened his shoulders and looked around in a business-like way. "Now, what shall we do with this little patch of land? The pavilion would go well over there, on top of that rise, don't you think?"

"You'll ruin the spot, then dash off to London so you don't have to look at it while *we* are inundated with gabbling tourists!"

"If it proves intolerable, you can come to London with me," he offered frivolously, then chatted on about his plans for the spot. "I'd like to put in some rustic sort of tables and benches for picnickers. Lovers who stroll about would appreciate a bridge too. Something romantic about a bridge, don't you think?"

"A bridge over the lake?" I asked, mystified.

"No, over the stream that runs at an angle down behind that stand of pines. Odd you did not know it is there, and you have lived here all your life. It shows how little the spot has been actually used or appreciated by those who are setting their backs up against its development. It is a small bridge I have in mind, not a great stone contraption like London or Blackfriars. Some sort of a garden too, something like you have at Ambledown, that thrives on neglect. An informal atmosphere, where beaux can pick off a bloom for their girls.''

As he spoke, a vision of the place began to form in my mind. He was not at all eloquent, but the simple, rustic nature of the park sounded rather pleasing. The place was pretty now, but impenetrable for long stretches because of the denseness of the trees, which is why I had not realized there was a stream.

''Any ideas to add?'' he asked.

''Perhaps some music in the evening—a few musicians in the pavilion...''

We walked on towards the heavily wooded area. ''Some of this will have to be thinned out,'' I mentioned.

''I wonder how it can be done without allowing woodchoppers on the premises,'' he replied, with a wise look at my change of heart. I immediately ran on to select certain favoured trees that were under no circumstances to be touched.

''I begin to think we ought to include a lemonade stand,'' he declared, running his hand around his cravat. I was becoming thirsty myself.

''Shall we eat now?'' he asked. ''I've worked up an appetite.''

My mind was running over the likely menu at home—nothing lavish on an ordinary weekday. When we resumed our seats in the carriage, he did not turn towards home, but went into town, to Wingdale Hause. I knew by his questioning face he was aware this did not please me. How could it, to break bread under the roof of my enemy? I maintained a ladylike silence (for there was really no better eatery in the village) as we entered the portals.

''It's really not a bad place,'' he said.

''Not at all. I always feel I ought to curtsy before Queen Anne's arms though. I wonder what she thinks of Wingdale taking them for his own, and putting them on ale tankards.''

''And pockets of dressing gowns,'' he added. ''I think it ought to be replaced with the Carnforth Arms.''

''What does that consist of? A Nabob rampant, crowned with guineas?''

"A Nabob couchant is more like it, with a spinster rampant."

It was all in fun, but it struck me that a Nabob passant would be more appropriate. Luncheon was edible. I'll say no more, except to add that liberal pourings of wine were necessary to make it even that. Wingdale came and joined us for a few moments, the ill-bred creature, to discuss business at the table.

"I've applied for enclosure rights to the patch of land across the lake from yours, Gamble," he said. "It will cost a pretty penny, but it will be a grand addition to the village. I don't see why Brighton should get all the customers that want to dabble their toes in the water. I am ordering a dozen bathing machines, and have got my eye on a few boats to hire out to tourists."

"You want to make it lively, Larry. Swinging boats of the sort they have at Bartholomew Fair would be popular with the young bucks," Jack said.

"Aye, they would, but they're not cheap to construct. I'm to build a little theatre you recall, for musical revues." The glance he threw towards myself told as clear as day these musical revues would be of a sort to make a Christian blush.

"I hear they have a very intelligent pig at the Booth of Knowledge at Bartholomew Fair, Captain," I suggested ironically. "Tourists would be willing to pay something to witness such a spectacle."

"If you hear of any counting pigs, I would appreciate learning about it, Miss Barwick," he answered good-naturedly. "I will have a Penny Pool too. Even servant girls can afford a penny."

"Pity you could not think of something to squeeze the ha'pennies out of widows," I suggested.

"I doubt poor widows will give us their patronage," he answered, in all seriousness. Gamble winked and suggested a maze might be good for business.

It began to seem the Captain would never leave our table, but when the tea tray appeared he arose and took his leave, to go and annoy other clients. No peace followed his departure, for when the tea came it was served in my own dear cherished silver pot. That wretched man had either got it from Tom Carrick, which I would not believe of Tom, or else my friend, in one of his piques, had returned it to Oldhams where Wingdale had snapped it up.

"Handsome," Gamble said, nodding at it. It was indeed a more handsome service than was at any other table, a special mark of respect from the host to his partner. "I have not seen this before. I wonder where he got it. An estate sale, I expect. A pity to see these old family treasures having to be sold."

"I saw it in the used article show window recently," I answered, and picked up my old friend to pour tea for us. I disliked to introduce any thorny subject over the tea cups, so waited till we were on our way home before taking Gamble to task for egging Wingdale on to such outrageous ventures as were discussed for his park.

"I wouldn't worry too much about it, Chloe. There's many a slip twixt the cup and the lip."

"At least it is a good deal farther from Ambledown than your park will be. I daresay we shan't hear the bucks drunken roaring, unless the wind is from the southwest."

"You would not hear it at all in London," he pointed out.

"No, nor in Paris either, but I don't plan to visit those cities."

20

WE LEARNED THE next day from Gamble, who found an excuse every two minutes now to come and disturb us, that the ruffians who had burned down our barn had been let off scot free. Lack of evidence, as I had prophecied.

"I shall certainly report this to the Chairman of Justices," Gamble said. I thought he was pleased about it, though I doubted any appeal would do *us* any good. In the long run, however, it might do something for justice in the community.

"How long is it likely to take before something is done, Mr. Gamble?" Nora asked.

"The mills of justice grind slowly," he admitted.

"Just so they don't grind to a halt," Edward said, in a philosophical spirit. His barn was set to go up the end of the week. Even now the raw lumber sat in the back lot, with workmen clearing away the rubble from the fire. It was impossible to forget Gamble had paid for it, and that we fell ever deeper into debt with him. It put a little constraint on the visits.

"If we had a more active Deputy Lieutenant, the case would be reported to him," Nora began, then turned rosy pink as it was borne in on her that we were beholden to our caller, the old earl's nephew. "How is your uncle?" she asked, to atone for her slip.

"Greatly improved. He's often sober for an hour at a stretch now, in the mornings. He promises to attend our ball. He is in high gig with all the company landing in for it. We have relations over from the western lakeside to stay a few days. Many of them I have not seen since I left home fifteen years ago."

One could only wonder that he would waltz out of the house and leave them so shortly after their arrival. Indian manners.

"Yes, Chloe, I am on my way back to them this minute," he announced, reading my mind. "You forget I have Mrs. Crawford and Emmie to play hostess for me."

"Lady Irene will be coming, I expect?" Nora asked.

"Irene tells me she never misses a ball, if she has to travel for a fortnight to reach it. She will be arriving for dinner tomorrow evening. I hope you will all come as well. It was not mentioned on your invitation, but Hennie has arranged a banquet of no mean proportions for a select company before the dancing begins."

Various sounds of approbation and acceptance showed our delight at this added treat. That we had been included at the last minute did not bother any of us a whit, for Hennie Crawford was held accountable for the lapse. Jack soon left on that occasion. The day was busy with beginning early preparations for the morrow. After Nora and I had given each other's face a lemon-juice rub, followed by cream to restore the juices taken away by the acid, I decided to try my hand again with the thugee rope. I never got to it, for on my way I saw the tinker's wagon sitting scraped but not painted. Its loss was felt keenly by Nora and myself, so instead I undertook to see to its refurbishing, including sending to the village to have a wheel made. This would not be driven to the ball. For that prestigious occasion we would take our own black carriage. The instant I opened the door I realized the stench of smoke made this impossible. It ought to have been airing out all these days, but no one had thought to do it.

While I stood wondering how we were to make the trip, Tom arrived. A servant came to me, and as I saw some hopes of going to the ball with him, I went quickly to the house. Nora was talking to him. I noticed she had stuffed her sewing under the cushion. What weaned her from her netting on this occasion was the addition of a row of lace to the bottom of her petticoat. I was impatient that Tom was so nice he would blush at this chore. In fact, Tom seemed very much of an old spinster to me, after the more roisterous company of Gamble.

"I thought your aunt might want a drive to the ball," he explained as I sat down.

"Kind of you to offer, but we are invited to dinner *before* the ball," Nora told him. My hopes for a ride with him were dashed.

"*I* am invited to dinner as well," he said proudly. "I chanced to be speaking to Mrs. Crawford and Lady Emily yesterday. Mrs. Crawford is a friend of my mama, you must know. She took Emily over to meet her. It was kind of her, don't you think?" We nodded. "While there, they invited me to attend the dinner. It sounds a very grand do. The Mandrels, who were to go with me, have arranged other transportation. So shall I stop for you and Edward, Mrs. Whitmore?"

"Chloe is going as well," she said.

"Have you indeed changed your mind, Chloe? Sensible of you," he said, but he did not fool me. He was not pleased. This mystery plagued me throughout the visit. Tom was not a man to be at odds with his noble neighbours, or to want his friends to be. Certainly his wife would be ragged to death if she dared to offend any prestigious acquaintances. He had disliked my refusal to attend. Why then did he not laud my acceptance more loudly?

We chatted about general topics—the fire, the rebuilding, and so on. It struck me as rather odd then that he had not come forward with any offer to help. He had been remarkably silent for a suitor, and remarkably little missed. When tea was served, he asked, "How—er—how are things between Edward and Emily?"

"How should they be, Tom? You know she is considering Gamble's offer of marriage. Taking her time about it, too, I would say. Edward seldom sees her, but for church on Sunday. Was she asking you about him when she called on your mama?" I asked, with more than mild interest. I had always thought she was too young and innocent to make a suitable bride for Jack Gamble. I think Jack was feeling the same way.

"No, she wasn't," he answered quickly. "She did not mention him at all, except to say he has quit writing poetry. She is sorry for that."

"I see." There was an idea so novel, so absurd really, forming in me that I was certain I must be mistaken. The idea was this: that Tom was beginning to entertain some amorous regard for Emily himself. She was pretty to be sure, and high enough born to flatter his ego a little. She was much too young for him—not quite eighteen, while Tom was over thirty. Still, age had not been mentioned as an impediment with Gamble, and he was a bit older than Tom. I decided to test my theory, and did it by stating what I thought he would dislike to hear, regardless of truth.

"I am not surprised she had quit speaking of Edward." He looked interested, pleased. "This ball will see the announcement of her engagement to her cousin. That is the whole purpose of it, don't you think, Nora?"

"I *did* think so," she agreed. "I recall we spoke of it some time ago."

Tom did not quite jump to his feet in protest, but he looked as if he would like to. "I think you are mistaken," he said. "Mrs. Crawford indicated nothing of the sort. She had hoped for a match, but her talk indicated the matter was as well as forgotten. In fact, she says Lady Irene has ousted Emily in his interest. It would be a much better match in my view than to shackle little Emily to him."

"What have you got against him, Tom?" I asked innocently.

"Bit of a ramshackle fellow," he said carefully. "I mean to say, there was the business of his getting some cousin into trouble before he ever left the country. Fifteen years out of the country will not have done his character any good, depend on it."

"He has been very kind to Edward," Nora pointed out. It was not hard to see she was piqued at Tom's words. Gamble had been inching his way into favour with her ever since the Indian blanket affair. Two evenings she had sat trying to remember some ill of Millie Henderson (the lady he ruined before setting out for India) without any success, though she remembered very distinctly she never cared for the girl in the least. Any man who accepts food and drink at the hands of a lady old enough to be his mother finds favour, so long as he does not treat her *too* much like a mother. There must be a little of the gallant in his makeup if he is to become a prime favourite. She could not like to condone these past crimes, but she would have liked very well to be able to forget them.

I chanced to remember, when I lifted the tea pot, that Tom had either sold my silver service to Wingdale or returned it to Oldham's shop. Either act was displeasing, and to tease him I mentioned it. I did not tell him I had actually drunk tea from the vessel but only said I had heard it was there.

"I offered it to you. You refused point blank. It seems to me if a lady says no she has no call to be throwing the matter up in a man's face. You would not accept it from me, as you have never accepted my offer of marriage," he said, forcing the words out, not without an obvious effort.

I really thought he had come to try his hand at weaseling out of his offer. Nora, usually so eager to throw us alone together, stuck like a burr. Tom resented it, but had he known the reason he would have rejoiced. The fact was that Nora was admitting, perhaps unconsciously, that she believed him to be no longer a real contender for my hand. She had said nothing to me, but it was there, to be inferred from her indifference and her not leaving us alone.

"You might have told us you were taking it back to the shop," I said.

"If you want it so badly, I daresay it can be bought from Wingdale. He would not know a Queen Anne tea service from a tin tray."

"He knew enough to snap it up in any case," Nora said.

"He is fond of Queen Anne," I said, and laughed to myself.

Tom was so unhappy with the visit that he rose to his feet. "Well, do you want to come to the ball in my carriage or not? That is really the only reason I came. I had a look at yours while I was at the stable, and know you will not want to submit your gowns to it."

"That is true," Nora said, looking to me for directions.

I disliked to accept so ungracious an offer; disliked even more to arrive at a ball reeking of smoke. "Thank you, Tom, we would appreciate it very much."

"Seven o'clock then?"

"Seven," we agreed.

I accompanied him to the door, in case he was dashing enough to broach the subject of marriage. And I would refuse him this time very firmly. He said nothing at all about it. Neither did he make any attempt at taking my hands, at touching me. He left with a stiff, angry face. He could be very unattractive when he pokered up in this way.

154

=== 21 ===

THE GALA NIGHT of the ball finally arrived. Tom called for us and took us in state to Carnforth Hall. More improvements had been made since our last visit. There was some attempt at shaping the shrubberies, and fresh pebbles had been laid to cover those spots where grass invaded the drive. It is one of life's little mysteries how it will grow so profusely where it is not wanted and refuse to come up on one's lawn, except in patches. Within, the changes were more dramatic. One had the sensation of entering a fine home, well cared for, with perhaps just a touch more of newness in carpets, window hangings, and sofa coverings than is usually encountered. There were splendidly-outfitted guests, most of whom were strangers to us. While Nora and Tom stood discussing between themselves which were titled and which less interesting personages, Gamble came forward to make us welcome. The strangers, upon introduction, proved to be friends and relations from the Western Lakes.

Entering the main saloon, I looked in vain for elephant feet, Indian blankets, and other objectionable bric-a-brac, to be told by the mind reader that if I had an umbrella I wished to store, I would find the pachyderm's foot in his study.

"You are looking very elegant this evening, Chloe," he added, scanning me quickly from head to toe.

"I had thought so till I got here," I admitted, for I am sure he knew it anyway. "I see you, too, have got a new bib and tucker for the occasion."

"Like it?" he asked, brushing his lapel and looking down at himself.

It was a handsome suit. There is nothing like a black jacket and white cravat to bring out the best in a man. Edward, too, was looking very aristocratic. Even Tom had less the air of a country squire than usual.

I felt the evening was going to be wonderful. There was champagne, an unaccustomed luxury in our simple lives. Lady Emily was beautiful in a white gown with silk roses catching up the skirt in ruches. When she smiled at Edward I did not see how he could well resist her, but his attention had been caught by a businessman from the west who was enlightening him as to the best way to invest his spare capital. Edward listened as closely as if he had a thousand guineas to dispose of. It was for Tom to do the pretty with Emily. I watched him closely. There was surely love shining in his eyes, and as surely none being returned by hers. Dinner, when it was served, proved to be no less than a banquet, with every manner of delicacy. I thought with dismay of the meager dinner we had served Jack at Ambledown. But we had not called it a feast, nor been expecting company.

Lady Irene was set at Jack's right hand, some elderly aunt on his left. I was placed between Tom and a gentleman called Sir Arthur something or other, who mined copper, and spent the meal complaining of the high cost and low productivity of his workers. Despite these twin destroyers, however, he had a diamond twice as big as a cherry pip in his shirt front, and the lady who was his wife had a whole set of them around her wattled neck.

I was unhappy to hear Captain Wingdale announced, when the guests for the ball began arriving, but was glad he had not been invited to dinner at least. When the minuet struck up, it was Lady Irene who began the dancing with Gamble. Had the purpose of this ball been to announce his wedding to Emily, she would have been given the honour. This settled in my mind that there was to be no announcement made. If any serious attachment were forming it seemed Lady Irene was to be the lady, as Hennie had said. Mrs. Crawford happened to be standing by me at the time. She had removed her black mittens for the occasion, and had tried to alter her customary flavour with cloves. Onions and cloves combined, I learned, give off a worse aroma than onions alone. Positively pungent.

"Lord Carnforth is unable to come down, is he?" I asked her. We had seen nothing of him since arriving, though I thought I heard a song coming down the stairs shortly after entering. Death and the Lady it was, so lugubrious.

"He was brought down for lunch. It knocked him about so that he is resting." I murmured my regrets.

Her eyes trailed off after Irene as she spoke on about fatigue and old age. She became quite a pest to me that night, though it was Tom who drew her to me. I stood up with him for the minuet. As soon as it was over, Hennie ran up to us again. "Where is Emily?" she asked.

It seemed significant to me that he could point out the precise corner where she stood. Neither did I fail to notice his feet were soon following his eyes after her. Hennie's eyes narrowed in speculation. "Mr. Carrick is a good friend of yours I believe, Miss Barwick?" she asked.

"We have known him a few years."

"I have known his mama socially a little, but was never at Tarnmere till last week. A very fine estae," she said, making it somehow a suggestion that I was a fool not to nab it and a hint to know my intentions on that score.

What did one say to such a thing? "Yes," I agreed. "Very fine indeed."

"I wonder what the income would be on such a place. Not a penny under five thousand, I should say."

I did not deny it. Her thinking was no mystery to me. Having lost out on becoming mistress of Carnforth Hall, she was thinking of setting Emily and herself up at Tarnmere. She would meet her match in Tom's mother, but let her worry about that.

Jack had spotted us and was fast approaching. "Chloe," he said, "do you think Tom would break both my legs if I asked you for a dance?"

"I cannot think so. He is not at all a violent man."

"I've noticed."

"Jack is always joking," Hennie told me.

"Especially when he is half full of champagne," he agreed.

She turned aside to speak to some acquaintance, and Jack

suddenly had me by the elbow. "We'll escape while it is possible to do so," he said, in a conspiratorial voice. "I don't wish to have my two duty dances in a row. I refer to Cousin Emily as the second, in case you wonder."

"Oh, I thought you meant Mrs. Crawford."

"Hennie don't dance. Her specialty is making others do so—to her tune. Having failed to bring about a match between Emily and me, she is now determined I must incite Tom to such a pitch of jealousy that he offers for her. I expect *you* would have something to say about that!" He regarded me closely.

"That depends on how you propose to set about it. I expect Lady Irene might have something to say as well," I countered.

"Was Hennie hinting it is Irene's mature charms that brought about the termination of the grand romance with Emmie?"

"Not in the least. She did not actually mention any termination."

"Well, I am mentioning it now. She turned me down flat, thank God."

I felt a weight fall from my shoulders. That match had never seemed a good idea to me. As the name of Lady Irene had arisen, I decided to discover whether she was in fact gaining any ground. "Lady Irene will make an unexceptional match for you. She will give you some of that quality you so sadly lack," I told him, with a pert glance that made it half a joke, a useful device for saying what we hesitate to advance in complete earnest but wish to get off our chests all the same.

The music began—a waltz. I had been half hoping for one, half fearing it. There were not a great many opportunities to practice this new dance (unless one were an habituée of Wingdale's soirées) so that I feared I would make a botch of it. Gamble's visits there had paid off. He could not have encountered the waltz before returning to England, but he executed it smoothly, flawlessly, while still continuing our conversation.

"Very true, she would take the edge of the savage from my social conduct in two days, but then she would also have to be the mother of my children, and the begetting of them with her is not a thing I anticipate with the least relish.''

"I'm sure Lady Irene is—is very good at it,'' I said, blurting out what I should have kept as an unstated thought.

"Too good, and in a lady, that is worse than no good at all, if it is marriage we speak of.''

"I wish we might speak of something else. Carnforth is *hors de combat*, is he?'' I asked, reaching for the first thing that came to mind.

When at last the dance was over, I looked across the room to see Tom mincing about like a dancing master, smiling and fawning on a thoroughly bored Emily. Bored with him, that is to say, she looked with plenty of interest out of the crevice of her eye towards Edward. Jack followed my glance.

"Edward had better look lively if he means to have her,'' he said. "Hennie is ripe for marriage. She'll talk Cousin into the first match that offers.''

"You have changed your mind about Edward's ineligibility, have you? Your first comment on that match used the word misalliance, if I am not mistaken.''

"I have changed my mind about a good many things. So has Edward changed. He is no longer a destitute poet, but a *reasonably* sane man of business. Ambledown is spruced up considerably—a home to be proud of, in fact.''

I wondered if the renovations at home had been urged on Edward with this in mind. "The sprucing up has put Edward considerably in debt. Emily has still no dowry. . .''

"How much must she have to suit for your brother?''

"You are the one who knows how much money he owes. He never tells me anything. And I was not hinting for money either. I am only pointing out that the match is as ineligible as it ever was—more so in fact. Nothing has changed.''

"It has,'' he answered reasonably. "I no longer mean to have her. And for my own part, I don't care a groat who marries her, so long as the fellow is not an out-and-out rotter. Unfortunately, all the matches trying to go forward here have one unwilling partner.'' His eyes slid warily towards Lady Irene, who watched him like a hawk.

"And in some cases *two*," I said, thinking of Tom and myself, who were about equally eager to be rid of each other.

"A pity we could not take a large wooden spoon and stir up all ingredients into a more acceptable form. There is Emily mooning after Edward, Tom mooning after her..."

"Irene chasing Gamble," I added with a laugh.

"And Gamble chasing you," he said, leaning his head down to mine. The air was crackling again. I felt suffocated with it. "Who are you hankering after, Chloe?" he asked.

"No one," I said.

"Liar! Ah, you lead a charmed life. Here comes Tom to your rescue. Emmie must have given him goodbye," he said, with a little ironic laugh.

Tom was looking piqued. Emily never minded her tongue, any more than her cousin did. She had no vice in her, but was apt to say something offensive through carelessness. In any case, Tom looked bruised. "Running back to Mama," Jack continued, ignoring my stiff back. "Kiss his wounds and make him all better, Chloe, like a good little mother." He fixed a peculiar, questioning look on me when I turned to hush him. The strangest thing of all was that I felt like doing exactly as he said, like patting Tom's head and soothing his hurt.

"But don't mistake your pity for love," he said, then stepped lightly away, just nodding to Tom as he left.

"Is something the matter, Tom?" I asked, sounding dreadfully like a mother.

Tom did not appear to notice it. "That Emily is a rude girl," he said. Clearly Hennie's plan for advancing his cause with Emily had failed. My closest questioning could not reveal what she had said. I sat out a dance with him, smoothing his ruffled feathers. He was happy to turn his talk to topics other than romance. After he had simmered down (it took two rapidly gulped glasses of wine to accomplish it) he said, "I was speaking to Wingdale earlier. *You'll* be interested to hear what he had to say, Chloe. He offered to sell me some shares in his place. What do you think of the idea?"

"How outrageous! He knows how we feel about that place!"

I answered hotly. After the words were out, I recalled that Tom did not share perfectly in my aversion to it.

"Just as an investment, you know. I would not be an active partner at all, standing behind a desk, or anything of *that* sort. He is in a bit of a financial bind, I gather, and is trying to peddle some shares in his business."

"I wonder his friend Jack Gamble does not bail him out."

"Exactly what I suggested to him myself. He didn't take to the idea one bit. Said something about Gamble wanting to take over. I ain't much of a businessman, but from what I gather, Gamble has already got close to half interest in this new village, and if more than fifty percent goes out of Wingdale's control, then of course he loses any say in what form the whole effort will take."

"Their ideas run side by side as far as I can see."

"Not really. Gamble has much grander ideas, or so Wingdale says. This business of developing the lakeside, for instance, came from Gamble. It is the heavy development of Wingdale's side of it that has got him in this tight money corner. Gamble urged him to make it a regular huge commercial affair, with swinging boats and a dance hall and lovers' walks—well he convinced Wingdale it would bring him a fortune, and so it would too, but in the meanwhile it has to be financed, and that is why Wingdale is after me for money. I wish I knew how much risk there is in it," he added, worried.

"Tom, you cannot mean you are considering going into this venture!" I exclaimed.

"Oh, deuce take it, Chloe. Someone will do it, and if there is a pot of gold to be picked up from it, I might as well have it as the next fellow."

"You men are all alike! You'd sell your souls for gold."

"Wouldn't go that far," he assured me, shocked at the idea. "I think the thing to do is to speak to Gamble about it."

"Would you trust him?"

"He is a gentleman at least. Mean to say Wingdale. . ."

"I wouldn't *consider* it if I were you, Tom."

"Yes, but you ain't me," he pointed out.

"No, it is pretty clear *my* desires have no influence with you," I answered angrily, then I got up, preparatory to flouncing out of the room but holding myself ready to be stopped. He did not stir a finger to stop me. I left, chancing to encounter Gamble while I was still on my high ropes.

"Don't tell me Tom has got out of hand," he said. "I haven't seen you look so angry since you rattled me off for going to fetch Emily home from your place just after I arrived home."

"Not out of hand in the way you think, but then his mind does not constantly run on lechery."

"Never wanders anywhere near it, I shouldn't think."

"You share something in common for all that."

"You intrigue me. What can I possibly have in common with that tame fellow?"

"Greed, Mr. Gamble. Greed. He would like to talk to you about the best way to get rich quick, without too much concern for anyone else's welfare."

"He's chosen the right man," he answered, smiling triumphantly. Before I could say more, he ran off after Tom.

22

I STATIONED MYSELF on a chair that gave me a good view of the parlour where Tom and Jack were having their discussion. I was positively aching to know what was being said between them, but was too proud to enter. I meant to nab Tom on his way out and discover whether he had decided to put his money into the venture. If he had done so, I needed no more excuse to turn him off. Indeed, his disregarding my wishes would be tantamount to his having rescinded his offer.

The two of them came out after about five minutes, and I arose to meet them. They were not looking towards me, nor towards the ballroom at all. They turned sharply to the right, to proceed to an even more private parlour—Gamble's study, it was. While I stood trying to work up my courage to go after them, a servant popped along carrying a bottle of champagne and two glasses on a silver tray. He took it into the study, indicating it was a long session ahead of them. In frustration I returned to the ballroom and got stuck to stand up with Sir Arthur, who was well into his cups by this time, and admitting he had made nineteen thousand pounds clear last year from that unproductive copper mine of his. One wonders how much he would have made had his miners not been lazy and overpaid!

After I had led a staggering Sir Arthur to a chair I returned to the hallway, to see the door still firmly closed. What a way for a host to treat his guests, to disappear for an hour and talk business. My next partner, Reverend Farrel, our minister, danced very much like a puppet, with little jerky, twitchy movements, frequently in unexpected directions. When the music stopped I again sidled towards the doorway into the hall, to scan that other, more interesting door. It stood open now. I walked quickly towards it, thinking to glance in, hoping for an invitation to join the gentlemen and be told Tom's decision.

Only Tom was there, sitting with his head at an odd angle. A closer look showed me his eyelids were also at a peculiar position, more closed than open. The poor man was on the way to becoming foxed, with all the champagne. He shook his head, and after frowning at me for a minute asked, "Chloe?" in an uncertain voice.

"What have you decided?" I asked, rushing to him.

"Eh?" he asked, shaking his head.

"About Wingdale. What have you decided? What did Gamble have to say?"

"Thinks we would make an excellent pair," he told me, smiling foolishly.

"Who, you and Wingdale?"

"Wingdale, that commoner? Wouldn't have a thing to do with him, Chloe," he said, reaching out a hand for me, smiling more broadly and more unattractively than before.

"Tom, you are drunk," I was forced to admit. "You need air. I'll take you outdoors." There was a pair of French doors on the far side of the study. I went to open them before helping Tom up, as I had an idea all my strength would be required to pilot him outside. I gave him my hand to help him arise. He insisted it was not necessary.

"Not foxed, by Jove. Can hold my liquor," he boasted, just before stumbling into a table. He did not seem to notice when I took him around the waist to lead him out the open doors.

"What did Jack Gamble say to you? Does he think you should put some money into the village development?"

"Nossir, not a sou! 'Don't do it, Tom' says he. Called me Tom, Chloe. 'Don't risk a penny with that rascal' was his advice."

"He wants to take the whole thing over himself," I deduced, and did not hesitate to say aloud. I was half beginning to think Tom ought to put some of his blunt into it.

"That's true," Tom agreed readily. But then he was not

really in a state to know what he was saying. There was a railing waist-high around a little stone balcony we stood on. The moon was hanging low, as it does here in autumn, a round, fat, yellowish-orange moon, conducive to romance. It was about the only feature of the night that was. Far off in the distance a few lights glimmered. Their location told me they were the lights of Ambledown, though it was dark, and I could not see all the intervening terrain.

Tom leaned his hands on the railing and took deep gulps of air. After a few moments, he stood up straight, appearing to feel better. "Chloe," he said in a voice very unlike his own, though not at all in a drunken way, "you have run me round in circles long enough." He had reached that stage of intoxication where he could speak out firmly, like a man. He lifted his chin so high he had to look down his nose at me, and he is only five feet nine inches tall. "You must put me out of my misery. Are you to have me, or no?"

"No, I am not. I hope you remember it tomorrow, when you are sober."

"Chloe, my dear, you *must!*" he insisted, stepping forward to grasp my hand. Such a brash move would never have been made by a stone cold sober Tom Carrick, I can tell you. Even as he spoke, he slid one hand around my waist. I wrenched away, ready to strike him I was so annoyed.

"You don't want to marry me, Tom. You're half in love with Emily."

"Any man might be half in love with her. It has always been you, Chloe, no matter what Jack says."

"What does that remark mean?" I demanded, my ire reaching new heights.

"Why, he feels Emily would be much better...but there's no point chasing after a girl who calls you a pest after all. It is pretty clear she thinks only of Edward. You and I will deal very well."

"You really do me too much honour, Tom, to admit I will do very well as second fiddle to that—that saucy chit of a girl!" I glared, and turned to march away.

"Don't go, Chloe," he insisted, taking a rapid step after me to wheel me around, into his arms. His wine-drenched lips came down on mine. It was like being hit with a wet mackerel. I pulled violently away, drew back my hand, and slapped him as hard as I could. The smack echoed across the valley into the night. Tom blinked, looked first shocked, then offended. Finally some expression that resembled genuine anger took possession of his countenance.

"He's right!" Tom said. Before he could be asked to explain this cryptic utterance, he went on to do so of his own volition. "You *are* cold-blooded. And a dashed bad-tempered female to boot," he added, with a 'so there' look on his face.

I felt it was myself who ought to be storming away, but Tom beat me to it. He had a deal more gumption drunk than sober is all I have to say about it. Looking in after him, I saw him knock against the table again on his way through the study. I leaned against the railing a moment to catch my breath before returning to the ball.

As if this ordeal had not been bad enough, it was followed by a worse one. No sooner had Tom disappeared than Jack Gamble peered his head around the door jamb. He had been auditing the whole performance, *hiding*—there is no other word for it— behind the concealing wall of the study.

He stepped out on to the balcony, grinning like a satyr. "You told him, no mistake. About time, too," he remarked idly, with a glance up at the moon. "Nice night for a proposal though, don't you think?" he asked in a purely conversational spirit.

"Never mind grinning like a hyena. This is all *your* doing. Tom would never have behaved so badly on his own steam."

"I didn't think he did so badly, considering his condition. Naturally I would have preferred he left my name out of it, and if he had been wise he would also have omitted any reference to Emily."

"He behaved *abominably*, and you put him up to it. Don't pretend you didn't."

"He'll be worse after he's married to you. Even an old maid like Tom will demand you pay the piper then, you know. What's the matter, Chloe? Scared?"

"Of what?" I demanded haughtily.

"Men. Tom certainly implied you are not *warm* in your amorous dealings with him. He said nothing to lead me to expect violence. 'A very cold woman' I believe was the phrase employed."

"I should hardly be surprised *you* would be so low as to discuss a lady behind her back, but that you will tell her to her face does surprise me a little, I must confess."

"Very true, old girl, but you ain't wiggling out of it that easily. Five pounds says you were trembling in your pretty little patent slippers when he got right down to kissing you."

I drew a deep breath to steady my nerves while I considered the most quelling, cutting reply I could return to this brash, ill-bred piece of impertinence. "Just because I wouldn't kiss that sodden wretch, and with an audience crouching behind the door jamb. . ."

"You didn't know I was there," he replied reasonably. "There is no audience now, save the moon, and she is used to such carrying on. *I* am sober—more or less—and I say you are afraid."

"Disgusted is more like it."

"Scared out of your wits, and I shall prove it," he said, wagging a finger under my nose. He moved swiftly, placing his hands on my shoulders to pull me into his arms and lower his lips on mine before I knew what he was about. I was excited by the unexpectedness, the unusualness of this movement: I was not in the least frightened. There was no reason to be. He was rather gentle, whereas I had expected he would attack like a tiger. The pressure of his lips on mine was so gentle, in fact, and his grip so light that I felt I could escape very easily. I placed my two hands flat on his chest and pushed. I was surprised he fell back so easily, till I realized he was only rearranging his grip on me. The hands slid down from my shoulders to encircle my waist, crushing the breath slowly but surely out of me. I could feel a pulse throb in my throat, but I was more acutely aware of the bruising pressure of his lips on mine, so strong it forced my head back. Still I was not afraid, but only more excited than be-

fore. It occurred to me he was *trying* to frighten me by this barbarous attack, to prove he was right. When fear began to arise,
it was not fear of him, but of myself. I felt my blood quicken,
grow hot, felt myself clinging to him as hard as he was clinging
to me. I felt, in fact, as though I were going to burst. Then I let
my head fall back. The stars were reeling in circles above me, at
a wild, tilted angle. The lights of Ambledown seemed to join
the stars.

He lifted my head up, cradled in the palm of his hand, and
looked at me; his eyes, in the darkness, looked wild and
startled. "Well, I'll be damned," he said, and laughed.

That mocking laughter served as a dash of cold water.
"You're a rake as well as a scoundrel, Jack Gamble," I said
coldly. "And I am not afraid of you, so don't think it."

"You frighten me to death," he answered.

"And I am not afraid of Tom either, whatever he..."

"To hell with Tom," he growled, and tried to kiss me again.

I fought him off. He took the absurd notion it was a game,
till I used an expression I had never used before—in fact, one
whose meaning is not entirely clear to me, though I know perfectly well it is not a compliment. The stable hand from whom I
accidentally learned it turned bright red and stuttered an
apology when he saw me standing behind him. Jack stood back
to examine me, and discovered I was in earnest. I was curious to
hear what he would say, whether he would have the decency
to apologize.

"You could be quite a woman if you let yourself, Chloe,"
was what he said. "Come, I'll see if the coast is clear for you to
go and arrange your hair. We wouldn't want the guests to know
what we have been up to."

"It would give them a poor idea of your hospitality, to know
you molest your invited guests," I returned, and brushed him
aside to go and tidy myself.

When I rejoined the party, the guests were going in for a late
supper. I went with Aunt Nora and some older cronies of hers,
thankful for the period of quiet to calm my spirit. My one wish
was to leave the Hall, but with so unusual and delightful a treat

as a ball in progress, it would be too hard on Edward and Aunt Nora to suggest it. Instead, I went back into the ballroom for more dancing, and ended up staying till the last dog was hung, as the saying goes. I had a very good time, too, as the host did not further molest me, but contented himself with casting secretive smiles at me from time to time, between dances with all the youngest, prettiest girls at the party.

I managed to do better for myself with partners than Sir Arthur and Mr. Farrell during the latter part of the evening. Several of Gamble's relations from the west discovered me. One of them told me thrice in the space of a single dance that he was engaged to be married in a week's time. Why he felt it necessary to impart this information I cannot imagine, but another of them was better company. He said the girls from Grasmere were much prettier than those from his own district, taking pains to smile all over me as he said it, to ensure my recognizing it as a compliment to myself, and not just the district.

As we took our leave (it was after three), Gamble was doing the pretty at the front door, and thanked me for a most enjoyable evening. Without batting an eye I told him I had not so enjoyed myself since he had been kind enough to escort me to Wingdale Hause to chaperone Emily and himself, and be insulted by the Captain. His reply, muttered under his breath, was fortunately not overheard by Nora, who is not accustomed to hear gentlemen use foul language in public.

You are perhaps wondering whether Tom was sober enough to take us home. He wasn't. He slept it off at the Hall, while we returned to Ambledown with other neighbours.

== 23 ==

I ANTICIPATED SOME lively doings the next day. Tom would call to apologize, and to have confirmed that he had been turned off. Hardly a pleasant visit, but it would bring relief. Mr. Gamble would call either to apologize or continue his impertinences. There was even a little suspicion that the cousin from the western lakes might pop in to say goodbye. None of these gentlemen appeared on our doorstep. Who came, at about four in the afternoon, was Captain Wingdale. That man has the nerve of a canal horse. He thought the gift he carried under his arm would assure him a warm welcome. My silver tea service it was. It was only my rampant curiosity that allowed him into the saloon at all. It was the first time he had ever called on us.

It is not easy to overlook a parcel two feet long and eighteen inches high. This had to be explained, even before he took a seat. He handed it to me, with a rehearsed speech that came out in a singsong "Pray accept this token of my esteem, along with my apologies. Had I imagined for a single moment this lovely treasure was yours, Miss Barwick, nothing could have prevailed upon me to buy it."

The urge was strong to throw it in his face, equally strong to snatch it while I had the chance and set it back on the sideboard in the dining room. As I remembered that it was this two-faced man who had arranged for a fire to be set to our stable, I accepted it with no feeling that I must offer recompense.

"Thank you. That is civil of you, Captain. Won't you be seated?"

He sat down, looking somewhat put out at my chilly gratitude "Was there any other reason for your call?" I asked, making it perfectly clear I did not consider this a social occasion.

"There is," he said at once, in eager accents. "It is about Mr. Carrick, if I may be so bold, ma'am."

"Indeed?" I asked, staring at his presumption.

"Your good graces could go a long way in convincing him to do what is to his own *great* advantage. Monetary advantage, I mean."

"So I assumed," I remarked, my sneer telling him that when Captain Wingdale opened his lips, one expected to hear money mentioned. He refused to take offence.

"He would come in on the development on your say so, I am convinced, Miss Barwick."

"I do not have the influence with Mr. Carrick you seem to presume."

"Oh, but you do. He said most definitely he had to consult Miss Barwick on the matter. Let me outline a little what I have in mind," he began, and pulled a stack of papers from his inner pocket. Without further ado he began opening them, first on his knee, but as they proliferated a table was required and provided. I was so curious to get this first-hand look at his plans that I submitted to all his vulgarity.

The original plan was drawn up in his own neat hand, a replica of it in the window of the newspaper office, and thus it contained no surprises. It was the scratched-in changes, mostly additions, that caught my eye. Neither did I fail to notice that some of these changes were in Gamble's bold, black hand. The version I saw had Ambledown subdivided into five areas, for five cottages. This got my dander up at the outset. When Wingdale saw his error in bringing this along, he took his pen and put a scrawl through it. "All that is changed, of course," he said hastily. "After your renovations there will be no reason to think of demolishing Ambledown."

"It would be impossible to demolish a property you do not own, in any case," I pointed out. "Unless of course, it should accidentally catch fire," I added pointedly.

"Shocking business, that. So happy it didn't amount to anything."

"I'm sure you are."

That sheet was hastily twitched aside. "Here is my lakeside pleasure park," he announced proudly.

"Ah, yes, the common land you managed to get enclosed. But surely the law decrees such land be used for agriculture?"

"Ha ha," he smiled conspiratorially. "Magistrate Muller is a reasonable fellow. He assures me there will be no difficulty. So long as it is producing revenue for the community there will be no trouble on that score. No trouble at all, if that is what causes you to be against Carrick's coming in with me, ma'am. I am ready to give my word on *that*."

He went on to outline the entertainment centre, each item of which would produce huge revenues—and huge crowds of riff-raff. "Mr. Carrick would be a full half-partner in it—that is to say, have forty-nine percent interest."

"Why would you be willing to forego such large profits?" I asked.

"It goes against the pluck to do it," he admitted, "but the work contracted for requires a down payment, and with my capital so heavily invested in buying a good many properties, I am short. A temporary shortage only."

"You could take a mortgage on one of your properties," I suggested, having a fair idea he was already mortgaged to the hilt.

"Mortgages! There is the culprit, if you want the whole truth, Miss Barwick. I have been lured into giving a mortgage on Wingdale Hause. Gave it to a friend, as I believed, and now he—he is pushing me for the payment."

The word 'foreclose' was carefully avoided. He did not wish to let me know he was desperate, his back to the wall, but the film of moisture on his brow hinted at it. He would never have girded his loins to approach *me*, whom he knew for an enemy, had his case not been urgent. I was in no doubt as to who his supposed friend was. Gamble, of course, held the mortgage.

"I expect you know who I mean?" he asked. I nodded judiciously, concealing my smirk at him and his difficulties.

"We are in this together, if it comes to that," he said, leaning his head closer to mine. I gave him a cool stare at this speech.

"I have a good idea of his business dealings. I know he has advanced large sums to your brother, Miss Barwick, and know why he had done so. Oh, he does not plan to tear Ambledown down, as *I* had intended, though I at least offered you a fair price for it. No, it is his wish to get hold of it for himself, to incorporate it into the village as a museum. Ambledown is the oldest home in the area. That is why he had it restored. He thinks he could charge half a crown for a tour of it, and tourists, you know, like to feel they are absorbing a little history and culture, as well as enjoying themselves. He feels it would give a little dash of quality to the village. He will have it in his hands by the year's end, unless you have some plan for your brother to repay those notes he has drawn from Gamble."

"Edward signed no such notes. Gamble is to be repaid in stock over the years..."

"For that fancy mount, yes, but the renovations to Ambledown were secured separately with a note. There is no point prevaricating with me, Miss Barwick. I was present when your brother signed. It was done at my own hotel."

"With your help and connivance, no doubt?" I demanded. He did not deny it, and I didn't doubt for a moment he told the truth.

"There was no thought in my own mind that your brother could possibly hold on to the place for more than a year. I wanted to buy it and subdivide. Gamble convinced me it would be better to restore it, and use it as a tourist attraction. He can be persuasive; he convinced me he was right, and suggested I use my money to open the pleasure park instead. Only it is much more expensive, which is why I mortgaged Wingdale Hause. I believe it was his intention all along to overextend me, so that I lose the whole."

I rather fancied this convincing occurred the night Gamble prevented Wingdale's men from burning us out entirely. If he were not a blackmailer as well, I would be surprised. Wingdale looked very sheepish.

"He has got *me* over a barrel too," he said baldly. "Our only hope is to pull together. If Carrick will lend me money to pay off the mortgage installments for a few quarters, I can go ahead with the lakeside park, which will bring in good revenues. Your friend will make a good profit.''

''That is no help to us in holding on to Ambledown. If Mr. Carrick wishes to invest his money, why should I ask him to help *you*, rather than us?''

''Carrick is full of juice. He can afford both. He will pay up fast enough if you will accept his offer of marriage.''

''Unfortunately, I have already refused him. Good day, Captain Wingdale,'' I said.

The man wanted to kill me. He had bared all his secrets, given me back my silver tea service, all for nought. He leapt to his feet, ready to attack, but something held him back. Some thought that I must now be forced to accept Carrick perhaps, and might still be brought to do what I was asked. He took a surly but not downright rude departure.

''Thank you so much for the tea service,'' I called after him, rubbing salt in the wound, and enjoying it very much too.

While the front door was still rattling, I ran to Edward's study to rifle his desk. His copy of the demand bill was there—fifteen hundred pounds we owed to J.R. Gamble, payable on demand. I could not but wonder what happened if (say when) we did not pay. The house was already mortgaged—he would not get the house, the bank would. Edward would be proclaimed a bankrupt. I supposed the house would be sold (to Gamble) to settle our debts. He would open it to tourist traffic—such dames as ''Lady'' Trevithick would be tramping through it.

The item of major importance and uncertainty was Gamble. If he held Edward to the letter of the note, he could ruin us. I was not so worried as I ought to have been. Somehow I had the idea he would come riding up on his mount and magically explain all his sins away. The more fool I!

— 24 —

I SAT IN readiness for Gamble's descent upon us, visualizing what form it was likely to take. If I turned coldly on him, would he get right down to blackmail? In my simple mind, you see, I thought an embrace betokened an offer of marriage, and naturally a man could not bankrupt his own bride's family. There was plenty of melodramatic daydreaming to be wrung from the circumstances. The prospect of being suborned into marrying the man offered the potential of a lifetime of being able to throw it in his face. As though his pride would ever tolerate such a thing! I must have been mad to think it.

One other episode occurred before nightfall. A note arrived from Tom Carrick. He remembered enough of last night to have composed and dispatched an insultingly curt note informing me he now considered himself free of any further responsibility to myself. He sent it with a servant, whom I requested to wait till I had time to return the insult. Mine took the form of expressing my delight that he had at last comprehended my true feelings for him.

Throughout the whole day Nora did not once pick up her netting. The blue rattan box sat forlornly at her feet while she fingered the copy of Edward's note for fifteen hundred pounds and made hieroglyphics on a piece of brown paper, figuring how we might pay the sum off from our income of five hundred pounds a year, quite three hundred of which went into mortgages before we ate a bite, bought a stitch of clothing or so much as a candle. As dinner hour approached, she had mentally sunk to dispensing with candles and lighting our home with rush dipped in grease, like the lowliest squatter who sits in his wattle hut on the commons. She was privy to Edward's chaotic financial dealings, but I did not wish to raise any false hopes in her that Gamble might be planning to save us by marrying myself. If I were wrong, I would have enough trouble without being a woman scorned into the bargain. As the hours dragged slowly by and still he did not come, my daydreamings were taking on a more sombre hue.

She had a high enough opinion of him that she did say occasionally, "We'll put it to him when he comes to call, about waiting a bit for the repayment of the note."

The reason Edward is not mentioned in this vigil is that he had taken to the hills to check the herd for some new misery that was going around, some pest that needed controlling. Ulrich had notified him of it.

"Maybe *you* are the one to mention it to him, Chloe," she said, frowning at her brown paper. "You have a better head for business than Edward."

I really could not imagine why he did not come. When Edward returned for his dinner, he gave us some inkling as to the reason. After telling us the doleful news that another dip might very well be required for our pesky sheep, he said, "One would take the roads around Grasmere for those of London today, with all the fine equipages trotting along. Gamble's guests leaving, of course."

This caused me to think Jack had been unable to leave them to come to me, and also to wonder whether the evening might not see the greater part of them gone, which would leave him free to call. As eight turned to nine, and (what seemed like twenty hours later) to ten, I was forced to admit he had no notion of coming near us.

The next day saw an interesting development in the village— one that affected us all—but we only heard of it in the streets, like everyone else. It was one of those momentous announcements that comes only once or twice in a lifetime and is greeted with about half the reverence of the instituting of a new monarch. Lord Carnforth had stepped down as our Deputy Lieutenant, and in his stead Mr. J.R. Gamble had been assigned to the post. He was to be the new chief executive authority and head of all the magistrates in our county. That same day, Magistrate Muller discovered himself too old to carry on, and tendered his resignation. It was generally considered this was done to save him the embarrassment of being removed from office. I waited in hourly expectation of hearing that the culprits who had burned down our barn had been re-arrested, but by that time they had gotten far enough away that they could not be discovered. The town held its breath to learn who the new magistrate would be.

I was familiar enough with the character of Tom Carrick to know he would not refuse the offer. Indeed, he would have done better than anyone else I could think of. I will grant him a sense of justice and enough common sense to carry out the job, even if I personally cannot care for him. What we have here is not an unpaid Justice of the Peace but a Stipendiary Magistrate, and though Carrick had less need of the stipend than most, he would have enjoyed the consequence of being addressed as His Honour Judge Carrick. Tom's was the name, the only name, being bruited about town in any case.

Captain Wingdale looked very worried indeed. It need hardly be said that Judge Carrick would not care to be half-owner of a shady pleasure park that offended so many citizens. I did not happen to overhear the exchange, but Miss Johnson told us that Tom Carrick had said in a loud voice within the Captain's hearing that if *he* were Judge, he would certainly look into such havey-cavey goings-on as having nightly assemblies. If there wasn't a law against it there ought to be, he said, for it was known to disturb the peace of the year-round inhabitants, and why should the entertainment of a parcel of tourists take precedence over the regular owners and taxpayers of the district? That Tom's speech was taking this judicial accent led me to believe Jack must have been sounding him out on the appointment, possibly in payment for not lending Wingdale the money he had requested.

And still the next day and night Jack did not come to call.

Emily did, *sans* chaperone. She came so close to dinnertime we were obliged to either let our dinner grow cold, or ask her to join us. I think the saucy girl put off her visit till she saw Edward coming home down the fells, which are visible from the Hall. She spent her time gazing at Edward, and gave us not a shred of hard news that we had not already picked up in the village.

It was Nora who asked her point blank if Tom was to be our new Stipendiary Magistrate. "Cousin John did not say so," she answered carelessly.

"What *did* he say?" Nora asked, driven to this frank extremity.

"He told me to put on my prettiest gown and come over, before Aunt Crawford decided to come with me," she admitted, and laughed gaily in Edward's direction.

Nora and I had been pinching at him, verbally chastising him for being such a wet goose as to have signed demand bills when he had not a guinea in the bank with which to repay them. He assured us no demand would be made, which earned him the title of simpleton. All our nagging had him down at the mouth, but other than that I think he was inclined to honour Emily with an offer. At such a tender age, a young gentleman is easily ensnared by an Incomparable. I was so vexed to see her throwing her cap at him again that I did not join the others in the saloon after dinner, but went outside to catch the nightly performance of my friends, the cardinals. Those artful, beautiful creatures must have read my wishes. They selected the most picturesque perches for their nightly song—low-hanging boughs—while they trilled and warbled to each other.

There I sat when *at last* Mr. Gamble came cantering up the hill. My heart tightened in my breast, while I prepared myself for some exciting interlude. "Good evening, Chloe, is Edward at home?" he asked, without even dismounting.

"Come to haul Emily home again?" I answered in the same casual manner. "You will find Edward with her in the saloon."

"It's just Edward I have to see."

"It is about payment for your demand bill then, I gather?"

That finally got him to do more than glance at me as if I were a stranger. The look he turned on me held much in it of hate. It was a cold, hard look, full of animosity. I was astonished. "Can it be possible you have condescended to speak to Captain Wingdale?" he asked.

"It seemed hard to turn him from the door when he came from the village especially to see me. But you need not squirm, Jack. I have not used my powers to get Tom to bail him out. I expect you will be able to foreclose on his mortgage, unless he succeeds with someone else. Pity he had not asked Sir Arthur. He'd skin his mother to make a profit."

"Which powers are these you speak of? Mr. Carrick's last heard opinion of you did not lead me to believe you held power to do anything but annoy him."

"That would be *after* you bribed him with the position of Magistrate for the County, I expect."

"He didn't need any bribing," he answered, and cantered on around to the stable.

I was sorry to see him go so soon. I had hoped to get in a few jibes about his museum before he left. I was strongly tempted to run after him and do it. He had come home from India, raising hopes that he would take hold of things, and he had done so, but in such a selfish way that we were in worse straits than before. It would be he rather than Wingdale who owned the new village. That was all. He would never tear down the expensive Wingdale Hause. He would go on running it as before, posting up bills to advertise his lakeside park and his museum. He would somehow get Wingdale's waterside property from him, as he got everything else. As our Deputy Lieutenant, there would be no stopping him. Soon he would be Lord Carnforth as well, to lend distinction to his vulgarities.

As the shadows stretched longer and the sun sank lower, I finally decided to go inside and see what was going on. Clearly Mr. Gamble had no intention of coming back out to speak to me in private.

There was a celebration in progress in the saloon, to which no one had bothered to invite me. That Nora had brought wine up from the cellar in lieu of serving either her home-made cordial or our ale informed me it was a major celebration. To see Emily smiling so comfortably made me think it was perhaps a betrothal that was being drunk.

Edward, looking towards the doorway, was the first to see me. "Chloe, come and congratulate me," he beamed. I noticed some new look about him. To put it more clearly than that would be difficult, but he no longer wore the air of a country squire. He looked more dignified. Even in the midst of his celebrating there was a stern, older expression on his face. Had the role of groom descended on him with such force? I would have expected a little more gallantry, more romance, to be in evidence.

"Tell me what the occasion might be, and I shall be happy to join you."

A glass was put into my hand by Nora, filled up by Edward, and smiled on by Emily in such a way I felt sure that she was ready to be a bride, whatever Edward felt about being a groom. As no one gave me the toast, I looked to Gamble, to see him examining me in a questioning way.

Edward cleared his throat, threw back his shoulders, and addressed me in majestic accents. "I have been asked to assume the position of Magistrate for the County, Chloe," he said. My confusion fell away in a flash. It was a *judicial* face he wore. Coming so unexpectedly it had not been recognized, but it was well done. "A great surprise and honour, for which I am very grateful to Jack." He nodded with grave dignity to our guest.

"You must be joking!" I exclaimed, without thinking. "Surely Tom Carrick will be the new Magistrate."

The Judge cast a sad, disapproving countenance on this unthinking remark. "Many will say so," he allowed. "I confess I had thought myself it would be Tom. I did not look for this honour, but when Jack explained it to me I could not refuse to do my duty, even though I am lacking in years and experience."

"What manner of explaining did Jack do to convince you you are ready to turn Judge?" I demanded, flinging the question into the air midway between the donor and recipient of the honour.

"Tom is a relative newcomer amongst us—not so well known

and established as the Barwicks, Chloe. The Barwicks have been here forever—longer than the Gambles, if it comes to that. I am familiar with the local customs, and as Jack says, justice must not only be done, but it must be *seen* to be done. That calls for a local resident of long standing. Everyone knows the name of Barwick can be trusted.''

"You are only twenty-four years old, Edward. You are young for this position.''

He nodded with a tolerant face. "True. Perfectly true, but who else would you give the post to? Not Captain Wingdale, obviously, nor any of those who have thrown in their lot with him. It must be a man of letters. I am better trained than a mere teacher or clerk. One of the few who have been to university actually.''

"Oh, Edward, you are too young. And a bachelor. . .''

Some expectant pause in the listeners told me I erred here. Emily stepped forward, still smiling softly, to grab Edward by the hand. "We are going to be married right away, Chloe,'' she said. Her voice was transformed to an echo with bliss. "Very soon, before Papa dies,'' she added shamelessly, "for if that happens first, you must know, we would have to wait for *ages*.''

"Surely you don't *disapprove* of the appointment?'' Gamble asked, his eyes wide in disbelief.

"I am too shocked to either approve or disapprove,'' I answered truthfully. Of course, it did not take me long to approve, once an inkling of the benefits washed over me. The salary was of importance certainly, but equally pleasing was to garner a little of my family's faded glory back again. My father had been Magistrate, and his father before him. Edward would hire a bailiff to help run Ambledown, and could stop playing at sheep farmer, a role that did not suit him perfectly. He was young to become so earnest and serious, but it was a role he could grow into, not one that would stifle his development. As I looked at him again, to see him in his new guise, the traces of youthful happiness were beginning to peep out at the corners of his stern lips, in little smiles at Emily.

I was so happy for him I ran to give him a kiss on the cheek, and with Emily so close to hand, she too received one. "Very best happiness to you both," I said.

"We'll be sisters, Chloe," Emily sighed joyously. "Isn't it lovely? You must stay here with us a while after we marry, or Hennie will think to move in, and we don't want *her*."

"A while" had a very temporary sound to it, but it was not the time to discuss that. We drank, first to Edward's new appointment, then to the marriage. I believe the sequence ought to have been changed in deference to the bride, but she did not mind. Edward proposed a special toast to her alone. By this time, Nora was wearing a fatuous, bemused grin. She was not accustomed to much wine drinking. Neither was I, if it came to that. "A toast to Black Jack Gamble!" she declared, with a nervous giggle at her daring.

"Where the devil did you hear that old name?" he asked.

Edward quickly seconded the toast, and we drank once more. Just before Nora's eyes began spinning in her head she excused herself to see to something in the kitchen, but in fact went upstairs to her room to lie down before she should fall down. I felt I ought to go after her and do likewise, for I was giddy myself.

Gamble leaned towards me, speaking softly. "It would be proper to leave these two old lovebirds alone a moment, don't you think?" he asked. His voice sounded far away, and hollow. It took me a moment to figure out what he meant, but I answered without revealing how badly my head was spinning.

"Certainly. They will never notice it if we step into Edward's study for a minute."

"I suggest we go out for a breath of air instead," he said, and took me by the elbow to go towards the front door. His strange smile accompanied by those telling words informed me he thought I was foxed.

"If *you* feel the need," I answered loftily, just before I tripped. The carpet does turn up at the edge, so I don't mean to imply I was staggering, or anything of the sort. Merely my head was spinning a little.

═ 25 ═

"THAT IS AN autumnal nip in the air," he said, as we stepped out into the darkness. "Do you want to go back for a shawl?"

"No, the coolness feels good."

"I thought you were looking a little flushed. I expect you have been wondering why I have not been here sooner."

"On the contrary, I was surprised to see you come at all," I prevaricated. I was not disguised enough to admit to any hope.

"I had several matters to attend to. When my appointment as Deputy Lieutenant came through in such good time, it made it easier."

"That was very sudden, was it not?"

"Not really. I set the wheels in motion as soon as you dropped me the hint Uncle had turned his duties over to Wingdale. My dash to London helped, I think. I tried to make the authorities aware there was some urgency in the matter, and it seems to have worked. I had the noose around Wingdale's throat pretty tightly already. He had spread himself so thin I was able to start squeezing him for monies owed. You are looking at the new owner of Wingdale Hause, by the by. We must change the name. What are your feelings about the Carnforth Arms? I do at least *have* a set of arms, so we can retire Queen Anne's."

"I trust you will change more than the name."

"The cook, certainly. We shall curtail their dancing too, but not eliminate it entirely. You will tell me how to add a touch of quality."

"I trust you are not thinking of redecorating it in the Indian fashion, with elephants' feet and hideous blankets thrown over everything."

"Oh no, I could not like to part with those cherished items. We will want them at home."

My heart beat a little faster. "A pity Lady Trevithick is not here to give you some suggestions. A museum room, perhaps. Or have you reverted to your original notion of turning Ambledown into the local museum?"

"Windgale let that cat out of the bag, did he? That must have been quite a visit. I did once think it a charming idea, but that is not why I set Edward to restoring it."

"I have been wondering whether you didn't do it to get him overextended, as you did Wingdale, in order to snatch it from him."

"Yes, I know you have. Your sharp comments upon my arrival told me so. Now, I trust, you have figured out the *real* reason."

His arm went around my waist as he spoke, making rational figuring of any sort difficult to accomplish. "You don't think I intend to hear for the rest of my life how you were *forced* to have me, do you? Whether you do or not, Edward's house is in order. What he owes will be my wedding gift to him, and his new position should bring enough blunt to carry him through till he gets his farm business in order."

"There is no reason in the world to marry you then," I said offhandedly.

I was suddenly and very violently crushed to a pulp in his arms. The fleeting glimpse I had of his face in the moonlight was dangerously menacing. If I had not been tipsy, I daresay I might have been a little frightened. "Shrew!" he said angrily, just before he kissed me. It was a ruthless, barbarous, bad-mannered attack that left me gasping, my knees turned to jelly.

"And *after* we are married," he said mildly, "we shall decide what is to be done about the havoc Wingdale has wrought in the village. Perhaps the original sheep farmers can be reinstated on terms they can afford."

"That demmed arrow-straight road..." I said, in a faraway voice, hardly caring two straws for it, at that particular moment.

"The weeds and grass will cover it in no time," he promised.

184

"We're going to make a great couple, Chloe. With your brains and my blunt, we'll keep all the Wingdales and other upstarts in line. If anybody tries to destroy our village, we'll have Edward toss 'em in the roundhouse."

"Is that what will happen to Wingdale?"

"No, it's not a crime to be penniless, and he's covered his traces of former crimes well enough that he'll probably get away, to destroy some other peaceful community. He'll walk away with *some* money, unfortunately. But I am feeling lenient tonight. I don't really mind."

We sat on the chairs beneath the beech trees, feeling rather than seeing the night around us. Our fingers were entwined, the mood benign. As my head cleared, I remembered to twit him about Millie Henderson, and he was lucid enough to exculpate himself rather adroitly.

"She wanted to marry a fellow named Billie Hall, and I wanted to go away to university. We got our heads—and that is *all*—together and devised the plan, got ourselves caught out in an *apparently* compromising position. Wilbur ditched her; about six months later she married Billie, and I was packed off to the East India Company school for Nabobs at Haileybury to study the four gospels of the Greek Testament, and translate Latin into English. Not a particularly *useful* course, but then it is good for a lord-to-be to have a smattering of the classics. So," he said, with a more lively sound to his voice, "how soon can we get married?"

"I think we ought to wait a few months. You have been in love with Emily and Lady Irene and the lord knows who else since returning. Better give yourself a little time to be sure this is not a passing fancy, don't you think? And I wish you will stop *torturing* my fingers," I said, as the pressure on them increased painfully.

"It isn't *passing*, Chloe. It was a while creeping up on me. Coming home to find a pretty little Incomparable destitute and nubile under my roof put ideas into my head. I am but human after all. Human enough to see she was only a ninnyhammer of a girl trying to make Edward jealous. I won't let on that was why

I made up to her originally, but I will tell you this: I knew the night I offered I would never marry her. So did she. We did not speak of it, but when she said Edward would be so jealous he would turn green when he heard it, I didn't think I would ever be her husband. I didn't give a damn either. I wanted just any respectable wife at the time. So I decided *you* would do as well as any," he added, and laughed tauntingly.

"Despite being practically engaged to Tom?" I reminded him.

"A lady don't stay 'practically engaged' for two years if she has any notion of marrying the fellow. We'll get married the end of September," he decided.

Emily and Edward came out looking for us. The Judge had decided it was time for Emily to go home, and for me to come inside. "Maybe sooner, if Judge Barwick proves too stern a guardian," Jack added.